Case Files of Bradley Kinkaid

By John Buckner

ISBN 13: 978-0-9978949-1-2
ISBN 10: 0997894911

Introduction

The afternoon sky was laden with dark clouds. It had rained sporadically during the morning hours and now the clouds were starting to form thunderheads. The weather was unusually warm for the middle of October. Most people were still wearing short sleeved shirts and shorts.

I was back home in Prescott after spending several months in Los Angeles working on a case for a client who lived in Prescott part of the year. It was a really strange case. My client had been reluctant to talk about it at first. I had to coax the details out of him.

First his adopted son had died some ten years previously. His wife had insisted that the son had not died of natural causes as the coroner had noted, but that he had been killed by the people he worked for. The wife had been seeking to prove her theory through supernatural sources.

When the husband found out about it he put a stop to her efforts, not to mention the large sum of money she had spent on the effort. This happened almost a year after the death of the son. Then to complicate the matter even more, the wife was found dead in her car in a shopping mall parking lot. The cause of death had been the exact same as the son.

The man had gotten on with his life until he started having dreams, or hallucinations, featuring his wife, still insisting to him that the son had been killed by his employers and that she had been murdered as well.

He tried to ignore the dreams but they were too realistic and the details stayed with him even when he was awake. He finally decided to have someone look into the matter.

I had just started an investigative business, having worked in counter intelligence in the military for three years. That experience allowed me to apply for an official license as a private investigator. He chose my name from the internet for whatever reason and called me. I listened to the story and frankly thought the man was a few cards short of a full deck.

We met at one of the Indian Casino's in Prescott for lunch and by the time we had ordered our lunch he had about decided that the story he would have to tell would not be very believable. He was right on that count and it took the better part of an hour to coax the story out of him. It was the first call I had since I set up the web site and I wanted to succeed in my chosen line of work, so I agreed to go to L.A. and look into the matter.

My thought was to spend some time looking into the things he had told me to give him some closure, never expecting to run across anything that would give the story any credence. I didn't believe in ghosts, or the paranormal if you prefer.

Much to my surprise, the further I dug the more the story seemed to have some basis in fact. I contacted a psychic who had also had some contact with the dead wife and after talking with her started to run down the threads I had come up with.

I still didn't have enough to really prove anything but someone thought I was becoming too nosey and tried to kill me. That sort of made me lean toward the murder theory. I hired a couple of unusual people in the local area and over the next several months put all the pieces together to solve the murders and implicate one of the employees of the company the son had worked for in a long running smuggling scheme.

The case had involved the local sheriff's department, the FBI and Customs before it was all over. I had gotten some good publicity in the Los Angeles area and told the people I had hired temporarily that I would try to expand the business in Los Angeles if they wanted to continue to work for me. All of them jumped at the prospect.

I had five young men, all black, and the psychic, who was an older lady, as a staff. In another odd twist, the man who had hired me met the psychic and the two had really been attracted to each other. I was occupying the house belonging to my ex-client and he was living with the psychic.

I had gone home to Prescott to pick up some more of my few worldly goods and would head back to L.A. the following day.

I checked my web site while in Prescott and had several inquiries from the Los Angeles area. I sent e-mails to the inquirers saying that I was out of town but would contact each of them within the next 48 hours.

Chapter 1

The psychic was actually a Doctor of Psychology and had made her living in the counselling field, although she truly was a psychic. That was what led her into the field of psychology. She wasn't one of those people who claim to be able to contact the dead on her own terms, but had enough experience with that phenomenon that she could actually be classified as a psychic. She was in her mid-sixties and had lived in the Los Angeles area for many years.

Merle Washburn, my client from the previous case, was a retired movie producer who had made a lot of money at his profession. He was also in his mid-sixties and had not actively looked for a replacement for his dead wife. The two had met when Merle flew to L.A. to personally thank those who had been instrumental in solving his wife and son's murders.

Merle had insisted that I stay at his house until I made different arrangements. I think the main reason was that it gave him an excuse to move in with Lillian Stutzman, the psychic/psychologist.

My name is Bradley Kinkaid. I was born and raised in Prescott, Arizona. I was a pretty good defensive back and got a scholarship to ASU to play football. After college I went into the army and applied for Officer Candidate School. I was accepted and spent two years in Iraq and my last year at Fort Benning, Georgia.

My move into the investigative field came about because I had worked CID in the army for two years and kind of liked figuring things out that other people didn't want known. Merle's case was my very first and had I not been anxious to get a start might have blown him off when he told me his story.

After I moved into Merle's house in L.A. I had gone to an electronics store to check into a method to see if Merle's house had been bugged. When I told the clerk what I was looking for he suggested that a friend of his might be able to have a professional look at the premises for as little as a hundred bucks. I told him to call his contact and waited for his arrival. When he walked in I couldn't believe what he looked like. I was expecting some small geeky guy wearing glasses. He was six and a half feet tall and weighed over 300 pounds. He had been an offensive lineman at UCLA and had gotten a pro contract. He had the sense to insist on a good insurance policy against the possibility that he might be hurt, which is exactly what happened. He got a good settlement from the insurance company but was not able to play football anymore.

He turned out to be very intelligent and good with computers. I hired him and as things got complicated on the Washburn case, also hired four of his acquaintances, all relatively young and competent in ways that I would not have suspected. We made a good team and they all seemed to enjoy the work so I told them we would try to make a go of the business in the area.

Merle had given each of them a $5,000 bonus and we would now have to start looking for work. Sam Rathbone, the big dude I was speaking of, lived with me in Merle's house, along with Irvin and James, two others that I had hired.

Irvin could do things with computers that I could only dream about. James, like me, was a veteran of the war in Iraq. He had spent a year over there and had not gotten a scratch. He started working for me and got shot before the case was solved.

Two others had been brought on toward the end of things and both were competent and didn't shrink from a challenge. I didn't know if I could generate enough work to keep everyone busy, but we decided to give it a go.

As soon as I got back to the house in Los Angeles I rounded up Sam and started returning phone calls. I used the speaker phone feature on my phone so he could hear the conversation but cautioned him to keep quiet and communicate by hand signals and facial expressions. I wanted his input if any of the potential clients should happen to require something that I might not be familiar with but he might.

It had only been a week since we wrapped up the case for Washburn and a major shootout with Mafia types had taken place at the very location we were still occupying. The end result was nine dead crooks with two injured and one of our guys got a bullet in his vest. Fortunately a county detective had been there when it happened and greased the skids for the investigative team.

I had gotten some good publicity in the newspapers locally and the national news channels had done live interviews with me and the detective. I didn't like the commentator and I guess that came across in my responses to his questions.

One of the messages on my phone had indicated that the person was calling because anyone who disliked the talking head as much as he did couldn't be all bad.

I called that one back first.

The man's name was Harry Clayton. He had not indicated what he wanted to hire me for but the area code was 714, which was Los Angeles County. When he answered the phone I said, "Mr. Clayton, Bradley Kinkaid returning your call."

"Thank you for getting back to me. I read about your exploits in the papers. I even watched the interview you did with the uppity newscaster. Did my heart good to see him put in his place."

"He had raised my ire by the way he treated the detective. I didn't really mean to come across that strongly. What can I do for you?"

"My daughter disappeared four years ago. The police have not come up with any clues and have no idea what happened to her. My wife and I have pretty much accepted that she was abducted or killed. The police say there is nothing more they can do. I wonder if I might hire you to look into the matter."

"I take it that she was in the local area when she disappeared?"

"Yes, at least we believe she was. We had not talked to her for three days before we discovered that she was missing."

"Where do you live?"

"On the coast north of Malibu."

"Could we meet someplace to talk it over?"

"Of course. Or you can come to the house."

"Maybe that would be the best option. When would you like to meet?"

8

"Whatever time is convenient for you."

"How about tomorrow around 11:00 am?"

"Let me give you the address." He quoted the address and I mimed to Sam that he should write it down.

"I will have another person with me and we will be there at 11:00," I said.

After hanging up I told Sam, "I don't know if anything will come of this or not. If the police haven't found anything in four years it might really be a cold case."

"I have found out from hanging with you this short time that the police do not always expend the effort that we will put into it. That's not a bad reflection on the establishment, just the shortage of manpower to look into things that show no promise of solving a case."

"That's true, but we need enough to go on to find a starting point. We will hear him out and weigh the possibilities before we make a decision."

I made two other calls to people who had left numbers. One was from a person wondering about security type work. He was a local business owner and had a rash of thefts and vandalism at his business. He wanted to talk about hiring nighttime watchmen. I told him that I would look the place over and get back to him within the next couple of days.

The second call was to an elderly lady who was having problems with her computer security. She had been the victim of identity theft on two occasions and wanted to put a stop to it. I figured Irvin could handle that one and told her that I would send someone out to talk to her.

I set the appointment up and then got together on the patio with Irvin, Sam and James.

To Irvin I said, "You are going to visit an elderly lady who has been the victim of identity theft on two occasions. I don't know if the incidents were reported to the police or not. You will have to pull the facts from her. I have a feeling that she maybe needs some education about computer do's and don'ts and probably an upgraded security system on her computer. The rule of thumb when hiring out our services is $50 per man hour. We are not trying to scam people so if what needs to be done can be done with a minimum of effort take that into consideration."

"Sam and I are going to the beach again. The case is a missing young lady. From what the man said she has been missing for four years and the police have no clues. I don't know what will come of that but we have a meeting tomorrow morning and should know more then."

"James, you can go have a look at the business of this gentleman," I said, handing him the address slip. "He has been having some theft and I think wants watchmen. Look the situation over and tell him you will get back to him after we talk about it."

When we got to the Clayton home the following morning I was somewhat surprised. The house was not right on the beach but across the coast road on a hill overlooking the ocean. It was a really beautiful view and the house was rather large. I estimated that it had at least 8,000 square feet. We drove in through wrought iron gates onto a circular driveway. There was a two car garage on each end of the house.

"This place didn't come cheap," Sam observed.

"Then he can probably afford us if we take the case," I replied.

I parked and the two of us walked to the front door. I rang the bell and soon a woman I estimated to be in her fifties opened the door. "You must be Mr. Kinkaid," she said.

"I am and this is my partner Sam Rathbone."

"Come on in. My husband is in the study."

She led us down a hallway and to the left. The study was at the end of a hallway.

As we walked in a man came from behind the desk and shook hands. "I'm Harry Clayton and this is my wife Roberta."

"Could I get you fellas a cup of coffee or something else?" Roberta asked.

"We're fine thank you," I said. "I'm Bradley Kinkaid and this is my partner Sam Rathbone."

"Have a seat and let me tell you the story."

Sam and I sat on a couch and Mrs. Clayton sat in a wingback chair near the desk.

"Our daughter Carolyn would be 27 years old now. After she graduated from college she took a job with an insurance agency. She wanted to become a financial advisor, you know, stock market and retirement funds. She worked in Pasadena and lived with us for the first few weeks. She didn't like the commute and decided to find a place closer to her work."

"When did she start working for the insurance company?" I asked.

"Late 2004. She graduated that summer and started the job in the fall. She took a graduation trip to Europe after school. Anyway she found a place in Westlake. In my estimation that didn't help much with the commute, but that was what she wanted. She worked for the company until she disappeared in the fall of 2005."

"How did you determine that she was missing?"

"Roberta had talked to her on Friday morning. We wanted her to come out here for the weekend but she already had plans. The two of them settled on a plan to have her come here on Sunday evening for dinner. We didn't talk to her on Saturday or Sunday. She didn't show up and we got worried that she might have had an accident or something. Roberta called her home and cell phone numbers several times but she didn't answer either. Finally on Monday morning we decided to drive to Westlake and see if she was home. She had given us keys to her apartment and we went inside. Nothing seemed to be out of place. We then called her work number and were told that she had not shown up for work that morning."

Roberta picked up the tale. "We were now beginning to suspect that something might be wrong and I wanted to call the police. Harry convinced me to wait until later in the day. When we still had no word about her at 6:00 pm we called the police."

Harry picked up again. "They met us at her apartment and we gave them the information for the missing person report. They looked the apartment over and told us they would check with the company she worked for. On Tuesday afternoon they called and asked us to come to the police station to provide additional information."

"Did anyone see her over the weekend that you learned about?"

"No one saw her from Friday night on."

"What do you want us to do that the police have not already done?" I asked.

"I guess I want you to go back and cover the old ground and try to come up with some clue as to what might have happened to her."

"Do you by any chance have a copy of the police report?"

"No. They never provided anything to us."

"I'm not going to give you a decision until I can talk to the police and look at the apartment. I will do that tomorrow. My basic fee schedule is $50 per man hour. I imagine we can do the preliminary work in a day. Once I see what turns up there we will make a decision as to whether we feel there's a chance of finding out anything the police didn't. If it looks as if there might be something we can do I will bring you a contract spelling out the particulars," I said.

"That will be fine. Do you want a retainer?"

"No. I will call after we look into it and we will talk about it," I said.

Sam and I left the Clayton house and went straight to Westlake. We located the police station and went inside. I checked with the receptionist and asked to speak with someone in the detective division.

Soon a plain clothes detective came out and asked, "What can I do for you?"

"I'm Bradley Kinkaid and this is Sam Rathbone. We have been retained by Mr. Harry Clayton to look into his daughter's disappearance some years ago. He said he had filed a missing person's report in the fall of 2005," I said taking out my PI badge.

"I'm Bill Hardwick. I've only been with the detective division a couple of years. Let me see what I can dig up in the files. What was the name of the victim?"

"Carolyn Clayton. She lived in an apartment on Westlake Blvd," I said.

He invited us back to his office and searched for the file on the computer. "It looks like we got the report from the parents. The young lady was supposed to have had dinner with the parents on Sunday evening and didn't show up. They called and didn't get any answer. On Monday they drove to the apartment and found things to be normal. She didn't show up for work at her office in Pasadena on Monday. The police talked to neighbors but nobody knew anything. It is still an open case but nothing has surfaced to give us a lead."

"Could you tell me who worked the case and how to get in touch with him?"

"You're the fella who was involved in the shootout recently?"

"Guilty. That was supposed to be payback for the smuggling ring we broke up but we got some warning that they might try something like that and were ready for them."

"That was a good piece of detective work running that down, and bagging a large group of the local Mafia wasn't bad either."

"I got some good publicity out of it and it appears that it is going to generate more work. The guy who hired me for this said he called me because he didn't like the newscaster who interviewed me any better than I apparently did."

"Yeah, I saw that. I thought you did a good job on him. I didn't like the way he treated the detective either. So what do you want from me?"

"I would like a copy of the investigative report. Mr. Clayton said he didn't receive anything from the police. If necessary I can get a notarized request from him, or just have him come in and pick up the report, whichever you prefer."

"It's still an open case, but I don't see anything wrong with providing a copy for the parents. I will give it to you to pass on to them."

He printed the report, which was only four pages.

"Nothing at all turned up in the initial investigation?"

"I don't believe so. Like I said, I've only been a detective for two years and have no first-hand knowledge of the case."

"I appreciate the help and if we turn up anything I will be in touch," I said.

Hardwick gave me a card and I gave him one of mine.

Sam and I left the police station and went to look for the apartment complex. It was not very far away and we simply did a drive by to get a feel for how open the area was and what kind of traffic was likely to be found in the area.

It was just off the Ventura Freeway and thousands of cars traveled the road on the commute to and from L.A. Sam had been looking over the report as I drove.

"Doesn't look as if they talked to a lot of people. I would expect them to talk to neighbors and co-workers at least."

"Possibly they did but didn't list all of them because nothing of interest came of the conversations. It could be that since the missing lady was over 21 they didn't attach a lot of significance to the missing person report the parents filed."

"What do you think? Is there any possibility of us coming up with something the cops missed?"

"I believe with the sketchiness of the information it wouldn't hurt to spend some time talking to the people who manage the apartment complex. There probably won't be a lot of long term tenants so it will be chancy trying to dig up anything there. The place of employment might yield some better results. It is at least worth looking into for a while. We can make some phone calls tomorrow and see if we can locate anyone who knew her. It would help to get an idea of her lifestyle. Sometimes the parents have no idea how their children live their lives."

"I know what you mean. My parents would have had a fit if they knew some of the stuff I did," Sam said.

"Call Irvin and see if he wants us to pick up some supper while we are out," I said.

When we got back to the house with supper we talked over our respective days.

Irvin said he thought I had been right about the lady with the identity theft problem.

"She is too trusting of her computer. I think I can spend a day with her and make up a crib sheet of do's and don'ts. That, along with a more robust security program, should keep it from happening again if she follows the instructions. I figure the whole thing for a couple of hundred dollars."

James said the man he had talked to about the thefts was indeed talking about night watchmen but he had about convinced him to install security cameras as a first step. "I told him we could install the cameras and equipment then give him a lesson in how to operate the system. He seemed to agree with the approach and I told him we would work up an estimate and get it to him. I figured Irvin could do most of that."

"It looks like we might be taking on a case of a missing young lady. We are going to do some preliminary work tomorrow and then have another session with the parents," I said.

"I guess that's not bad for our first day," Irvin said.

"We need to get listed in some of the on-line directories for the area. Can you handle that?" I asked Irvin.

"Piece of cake, but it's going to cost us, just like an advertisement in the yellow pages would. This won't be as expensive as print though."

I hadn't talked to Lillian for over a week so I gave her a call that evening. I told her that I would stop by the following day.

Sam and I had breakfast at a Denny's and then went to Lillian's house. She had a pot of coffee on and invited us to sit at the dining room table. Mavis, her friend from back east, had gone back home a couple of days before. She probably wanted to give Lillian and Merle some time to get to know each other better.

"So what's happening?" she asked.

"Sam and I went to the beach yesterday to talk to a couple about their daughter who has been missing since 2005. We stopped by the police station and got a copy of the missing person's report yesterday. We plan to try to talk to someone who might have known her from her apartment building. I told Sam that's a long shot. Renters tend to move around more than home owners. We are also going to Pasadena to talk to her old employer. If we turn up anything that looks like it might be something the police have not gotten wind of we will probably take the case to see if we can come up with anything worthwhile."

"Got a couple of more calls from people about more mundane things. Irvin is going to try to get us set up with on-line yellow pages. I really think most of the calls I get will be for lesser things, like divorces and stuff like that."

Merle asked, "Do you think you will be able to make a go of it here?"

"It's too early to tell just yet. Are you wanting your house back?" I said with a chuckle.

"Nothing like that. I just wondered if there is a large market for private investigators," he replied.

"There are quite a few listed in the phone book. I don't have any idea how much business they get. I am going to try this for six months and see if it works."

"Plan on staying in the house until the trial period is over."

"I can't do that without paying you some rent," I said.

"We can talk about that after we see how successful you are."

We stayed for almost an hour and then headed to Westlake again.

Chapter 2

When we got to the apartment complex where Carolyn had lived we walked around the area. I had gotten the apartment number off the police report but I didn't know which building she lived in. There were four buildings in a rectangular arrangement with open space in the middle. We just walked around until we found a sign leading us to the manager's office. We walked up and I rang the doorbell.

A middle aged man answered the door. "May I help you?" he asked.

I took out my badge and showed it to him. "I'm a private investigator. This little fellow is my partner Sam Rathbone. My name is Bradley Kinkaid. We are looking into a missing person report from some years ago. The lady in question lived in one of your apartments. Her name is Carolyn Clayton. She disappeared in late 2005."

"I didn't take over the manager's position here until the summer of 2006 so I don't know that I will be of much help to you."

"Could I ask you to check your records and see if you have anyone still in residence who was here in 2005?" I asked.

"I will need to look at the records. I have them computerized so it won't take long. What was the apartment number?"

"4217," I said.

"That would be apartment 217 in building four. The first number designates the building."

He invited us in and went to his computer. After a couple of minutes he said, "Looks like there are only a few people here now who were in residence then. I have one person in her building and four others in the next building. Let me get a print out of the ones who were here in late 2005."

He punched a few keys and the printer spit out the list. It gave the names and apartment numbers for each of them.

"Thanks. I really appreciate it. The police haven't been able to turn up any leads so we are hoping to have better luck," I said. "Is it all right to just go in and knock on the doors?"

"We have a no solicitation policy but I don't think you would fit into that category. Just knock and see if they will talk to you. If you wish you can tell them that I Okayed it."

We walked to the building Carolyn had lived in and located the apartment for the tenant. Her number was 4304. According to what the manager told us that would be building 4, third floor apartment number 4. We found it and knocked on the door.

An elderly lady answered the knock. I again went through the routine of showing the badge and explained what we wanted to talk to her about.

She remembered Carolyn. "She was a sweet girl. I used to walk some for exercise in the late summer and fall. I eat supper kind of early and try to walk a little of it off before bedtime. She used to walk some and we would walk together and talk."

"What time did she normally get home from work?" I asked.

"It varied somewhat but was usually between six and six thirty. I think she had a pretty good commute. If she got off at five it would take her about an hour to get here from Pasadena, which is where she worked."

"What sort of things did you talk about?"

"Different things. She had graduated from college and gone to Europe before she went to work. Apparently her folks are pretty well off. They live somewhere near the beach. She talked about them some. She had a good childhood from the things she told me. You can tell a lot about people's likes and dislikes just by listening to their demeanor when they talk about them. She seemed to get along with her parents and enjoyed visiting them."

"Did you visit back and forth in your apartments?" I asked.

"Not a lot. I was in her apartment four or five times. I had her to dinner a couple of times on the weekend. It would be really inconvenient during the week because I eat so early."

"Did she have any friends visit her?"

18

"I don't really know. I am on the third floor and she was on the second so we did not see a lot of each other unless we happened to pass going or coming."

"Any boyfriends that you knew of?"

"No. Like I said, living on different floors I would not be aware of any of her visitors."

"Do you have a computer?"

"No. I am too old to learn how to operate one of the things. I get along with my television and hobbies."

"How about Carolyn? Did she have a computer?"

"Yes. She had it set up in a corner of the living room and I did notice that. She didn't have a lot of furniture, but what she had was neat and well cared for. I never went into her apartment and found it messy. She kept the place spotless."

"What about alcohol? Did she drink?"

"I suppose she drank wine. I saw a couple of bottles on the counter one of the times I was in her apartment. I don't believe she went out drinking, but I don't know that for sure. She didn't talk about her love life to me. I don't mean that in the sense of sleeping with someone, just whether she was seeing someone she was interested in. She was really personable and had a good sense of humor."

"I'm going to talk to some other tenants that were here when she was. Can you recommend anyone who might know more about her?"

"Sorry. I am old enough that I don't do the stairs any more often than is absolutely necessary now. If it didn't happen on the third floor then it didn't happen for me," she said.

"We may want to come back and talk to you again if you have no objections."

"That's fine. Just knock on the door. I usually don't get out much, other than grocery shopping."

"Thank you again for your cooperation," I said as we departed.

We talked to three other tenants who had been there in 2005. All were in different buildings from Carolyn's. They all remembered her and had nothing bad to say about her. The police had not talked to any of them during the initial investigation.

I wanted to talk to all who had been there and the two who didn't answer their door probably worked day jobs and either lived alone or the wife worked too.

I told Sam, "We are going to have to come back in the evening to catch the others."

"You asked about the computer because you think there might be something to show others she knew?" Sam asked.

"You're the computer guy. Wouldn't it make sense to look at her computer usage to see what kind of things she was interested in? Also, if we can access her e-mail account we can find out who she corresponded with regularly. It may not lead anywhere, but then again it might."

"Wonder what the parents did with the furniture?"

"That's a good question to ask them when we go back."

"You think there might be enough to take the case?" Sam asked.

"I don't know. It will depend on whether we can locate her computer, and then what we find on it. I think we should go back and talk to Harry and Roberta again before we go to the company she worked for. It could be that some of the employees knew her better than her neighbors."

The next day we went back to the Clayton's after calling. It was just after 10:00 am when we arrived.

"What do you think," Harry asked after we were seated in his study.

"We found that six of the current tenants were there when she disappeared. One older lady lived in the same building but one floor above. She walked in the evenings at that time and remembered her because they sometimes walked together. She had only good things to say about Carolyn. She said they visited back and forth some, but not often. She indicated that Carolyn had a computer in one corner of the living room. Do you know what happened to her furniture?" I asked.

"It's in our garage. We hired a moving company to pack the stuff up and bring it here. It has sat in the garage since."

"Do you know if her computer was among the items they delivered?"

"I assume so. It was there when we went over that Monday."

"Did the police ask about the computer?"

"No, not that I remember."

"Would it be possible to get her computer so we can look at the hard drive and see if there is anything there to give us a place to start?"

"You think it's worthwhile to look into the matter further then?"

"I believe there might be something that will point us in the right direction. The people she corresponded with via e-mail and maybe an appointment calendar to tell us who she might have been in contact with that weekend, or prior. We didn't go to the place where she worked yet either and that might tell us something about her local acquaintances," I said.

"Let's go to the garage and see if we can locate the computer," Harry said.

He took us to the garage on the north side of the house. The entire space was used for storage and he pointed us toward the items removed from Carolyn's apartment.

It didn't take long to locate the computer. All the boxes were marked with the contents. Sam picked up the box with the computer and brought it to an area where we could open it. He extracted the computer tower. It was an HP, typical for home use.

"Do you mind if I take this with me so we can have our computer guy look it over?" I asked.

"Not at all. I don't know why I didn't think of that, or the police for that matter."

"I want to look at the computer and visit her old workplace before we make a final decision about how to proceed if that's all right with you," I said.

"You've already done more than the police did. I sure hope you can come up with something that will help us find out what happened to her."

"I will call you tomorrow, probably later in the day. I want to visit Pasadena in the afternoon."

Sam carried the computer to the car and we were about ready to leave. "Do you know of any friends in the area Carolyn might have had?"

"She grew up here so there are a good many acquaintances. I don't know if she renewed any of the friendships after college but no one came forward when the report was filed," he said.

"Could I ask you to sit down with your wife and make a list of anyone you remember as friends?"

"We will do that this evening."

I drove back to the house and Sam unloaded the computer. When we got inside I said to Irvin, "Got a project for you. This is the computer belonging to the young lady who went missing four years ago. See what you can find out about her from it. If you can get access I would like to have the names of everyone in her address book. If you can access the e-mails go over them thoroughly for anything that might point to a relationship or anything else out of the ordinary."

"I finished up with Miss Sizemore today. I believe she feels a little more confident now about her computer. I charged her $200 and she tipped me a hundred," Irvin said.

"Maybe you can get enough off this thing to give us a direction for tomorrow's activities. Sam and I are going to Westlake tonight to try to catch the two neighbors of Carolyn's that we missed yesterday. You guys are welcome to come along if you want."

"I think I will start messing with the computer and see what I can find out while you are gone," Irvin said.

James elected to stay home with Irvin so Sam and I had a quick microwave dinner and headed back to Westlake.

One of the neighbors lived directly across from Carolyn's former apartment. I knocked on the door and a lady who appeared to be in her forties opened the door.

"Good evening ma'am. My name is Brad Kinkaid and this is my partner Sam Rathbone. We have been asked to investigate the disappearance of one of your neighbors from late 2005. I know it is an old case but the police didn't turn up anything of substance to explain what happened and the young ladies parents hired us to look into the matter again." I showed her my PI badge.

She didn't invite us in but talked through the screen door. I didn't much blame her for the precaution.

"Is this the young lady who lived directly across the square?"

"Yes ma'am, that's the one. Did you know her very well?"

"Not really. I would see her coming and going at times, and we spoke when we happened to be going to the mailbox at the same time, or just passing on our way to our own errands."

"Could you give me your impression of her? I don't mean that in any derogatory way, just kind of a thumbnail sketch of her personality. Was she open and friendly, standoffish, or somewhere in between?"

"She was always pleasant when we spoke. She was a very attractive young lady and seemed to be from a wholesome background. Her parents would sometimes visit in the evening for dinner or just to visit. Our front window looks directly across into her section of the building. Not that we snooped or anything like that. We tend to leave our drapes open until we go to bed and the eye is naturally drawn to activity in the line of sight. She had visitors in the evening at times. Some male and some female. Like most of us who live here she worked days. I believe she might have been part of the white collar community. She had a college degree I think and seemed really intelligent."

"What can you tell me about any male visitors?"

"Not much. I saw men approximately her age visiting at times but I don't know if they stayed or not. We usually go to bed around ten and sometimes the car was still there when we called it a night but don't draw any conclusions from that," she said.

"She never had parties or large groups of people over?"

"Not that I noticed. Like I said, she seemed like a very nice young lady."

"Thank you for your time. We won't keep you any longer. If anything else comes to mind give me a call please," I said and handed her one of my cards. Sam and I then turned to the sidewalk to visit the other person on our list.

The last one lived in the adjacent building and we managed to catch him at home. He looked to be in his early thirties and worked for a delivery company.

I showed my badge and explained what we were looking for. He said he knew her by sight and had talked to her on several occasions and had asked her out but she refused. At that point he lost interest and didn't pay much attention to her. "I work long hours and most of the time it is after 8:00 pm when I get home. Our paths just didn't cross that often."

Once we were back in the car I told Sam, "I hope we have better luck at her former place of employment, or that Irvin comes up with something worthwhile from her computer."

"If there's anything there Irvin will find it," Sam said with assurance.

Chapter 3

It was almost ten by the time we got back to the house. Irvin was at the computer desk with Carolyn's computer sitting on a chair and plugged into Merles peripherals.

"Any luck yet?" I asked when I saw what he was doing.

"I got into the system but haven't made much headway yet. I just a few minutes ago managed to get access to her password. I'm going to stick with it a while longer. You guys try not to snore too loudly if you go to bed."

"You got it. Soft snores," Sam said.

Sam and I went to bed after having a beer on the patio.

When I got up the next morning there were several pieces of computer paper on the table with a note from Irvin.

The note said, *got access to her address book but not her e-mail account. I plan to call some of those on the list and see if they still have her e-mail address.*

I picked up the list he had left with the note. He had made two copies so I took one as Sam and I prepared to go find some breakfast. "It appears that she had a lot of friends unless some of these are professional acquaintances," I said.

Sam took the paper and looked it over. There were more than fifty names on the list.

"What exactly are we looking for here?" Sam asked.

"Someone who had contact with her after that Friday night. I would like to pin down the last time she was seen," I said.

We had a leisurely breakfast at the same Denny's we usually frequented. "I think the computer is going to be our best bet for finding anything worthwhile," I said.

"It's possible that someone from her company will remember something important," Sam replied.

"Ever the optimist," I said.

After the traffic cleared somewhat we drove to Pasadena. Her office was in a building of eight stories along what was the old Route 66. We found a visitors parking spot and went inside the building. I had the name of the company from the police report and we located them on the sixth floor.

I expected the company to be rather large and was somewhat taken aback by the fact that they only had about twenty employees. I don't know what I expected but that wasn't it.

I asked the receptionist if I could talk to the manager of the firm and she called him on an interior line.

He came out to meet us and I introduced Sam and myself.

"We are looking into the disappearance of a young lady who worked for your firm in the fall of 2005. The police in Westlake investigated the case and no evidence came to light about what happened to her. Her parents hired us to go over the case again just to be sure something was not missed."

"That's almost five years ago. We probably only have a few people who were here then. I am new to the area, at least in terms of being employed here," he said.

"Would it be possible to talk to those who were here at that time to try to get a thumbnail sketch of her personality?"

"Sure. Let me point them out to you."

He asked the secretary/receptionist for a personnel roster and then went over the list with her to indicate which were there in 2005. The number was less than ten.

We talked to all of them for a few minutes each. The opinions were all of a positive nature. She was well liked and seemed very competent about her work. Nobody knew of any drinking habits or had ever had discussions about men friends.

Also of note, none of them had seen her on the weekend she disappeared.

The group consisted of four younger females, all I estimated to be under thirty, two men, both in their forties, and three older females. It didn't look as if this was going to be of much help.

None of the people we talked to socialized with her outside work. They mostly lived in the Pasadena area and with her in Westlake it was not likely that their paths would have crossed after work unless it was a company sponsored event. I asked about those too and learned that they only had a single social event annually and that was a Christmas party.

Sam and I headed back to L.A. It appeared that our only hope was to find something on her computer to give us a nudge in the right direction. I said as much to Sam.

"If there's anything there Irvin will find it eventually. Why do you come up with these cases that are older than I am?" he asked.

"Because if they were easy the cops would already have solved them," I said.

We got back to the house at lunch time. The trip to Pasadena hadn't taken long at all. Irvin was still on Carolyn's computer.

"Any luck?" I asked.

"Some. I got her e-mail address from one of her acquaintances and I am trying to get into that now," he answered.

"How are you going about that?"

"Trying combinations of her personal profile. Birthdate, where she was born, social security number; things like that."

"Is that going to take a lot of time?"

"It's hard to say. She could have made it a lot easier if she had asked the computer to remember her password. Most e-mail accounts are set up to give you a clue if you enter the data wrong a couple of times. Hers didn't do that so she was a bit more security conscious than most people."

"We struck out at her workplace. There were several people there who remembered her and they all had nice things to say. Unfortunately none of them saw her the weekend she came up missing," Sam said.

"How many of her friends have you called and what kind of questions did you ask them?" I asked.

"I only called one. It was a female friend and she still remembered the e-mail address. That was all I asked, after telling her why I wanted the address," Irvin said.

"Then I think you and I have our work cut out for us this afternoon," I said to Sam.

"All the addresses have phone numbers with them but remember that the information is five years old and might not be valid any longer," Irvin said.

The middle of the afternoon was not the best time to catch people who worked at home as we very quickly found out. Sam and I had split the list and moved to different areas for some privacy for the calls.

I started at the top of my list and found that my assumption about people not being available during working hours was pretty valid. I got answering machines more often than not and some of the phones were no longer in service, or had been assigned to someone else. Fortunately there were some cell numbers and I had better luck with those.

One was a friend, Pamela Whitehead, she had known growing up and when I explained what I was attempting to do was very cooperative.

"Did you see her often after she came back here to work after college?" I asked.

"Not like when we were teenagers, but at least once a week, sometimes more often."

"What kind of setting? Did you dine together, have drinks, double date? Anything of that nature?"

"I would visit her at her apartment and sometimes we would have a glass of wine but neither of us were real drinkers."

"When was the last time you saw her?"

"I saw her the Saturday evening before her parents reported her missing on Monday."

"Would it be possible to meet so I can get some additional information?" I asked.

"I suppose so. What do you have in mind?"

"I don't have an office but I work with a psychologist in the area and I would like her to sit in on our conversation if you wouldn't mind. I will need to coordinate it with her. What day and time is most convenient for you?"

"I work from eight to five and my commute is not a long one, so any time after 7:00 p.m. would be fine. Tomorrow or the next day would also work."

"She lives in Burbank, is that near you?"

"Not too far away. I still live near the beach so it shouldn't take me more than half an hour to get there in the evening hours."

"I will set it up with Lillian and call you back," I said. "I really appreciate your cooperation."

"If it will help you find out what happened to her I am glad to do it."

After I hung up I immediately called Lillian and told her what I had in mind. "I want to interview the young lady in your presence. I know it is like a shot in the dark but I want to see if you get any psychic vibes from her."

"I wouldn't count on that. You know that the spirits are the ones who choose to make contact, not the other way around."

"I know, but I keep thinking about your experiences you related about your youth and how your group approached the problem. Seems that all the contact you had was from people in stressful situations when they died. If there's even an outside chance I want to make sure the opportunity is presented," I said.

"Stranger things have happened," she said. "When do you want to meet?"

"How about tomorrow evening around 8:00 p.m.?"

"I will be ready. Do you want Merle in on this?"

"If he wants in. I don't want him to feel obligated but another perspective is always welcome."

I then called Pamela, the lady in question back and gave her the address and time for the meeting.

I only managed to contact three other people from the list and set up a time to call on one of them. The other two were not very close to her and didn't think they would be able provide any information that would help the case. I always wondered why people said they couldn't add anything to help when they didn't know what would be beneficial and what wouldn't.

Irvin, meanwhile, was still trying to get access to her e-mail account. If he could get into that he could call up her erased messages and might have some luck there. He was getting tired of messing with the e-mail problem and decided to look at the other stuff on her computer just to take a break.

He went to her word processing program and looked it over. It didn't have a separate password and all the documents were there for the viewing. He scrolled through the list of files. There were letters to friends, who apparently didn't do much with computers, otherwise the letters would have been e-mails.

He found one labeled, 'diary' and opened the file.

It was rather lengthy and started in the year 2000, about the time she would have started to college. He skimmed some of the entries briefly and made a note to copy the file and have Sam and Brad read it thoroughly. This was the sort of document that might yield some worthwhile information if she was like most young women.

He went ahead and made two copies of the file, on separate discs, so they could all work simultaneously.

Sam and I soon met at the kitchen to get drinks and Irvin said, "I found something that might be worthwhile looking at. It's a diary in a word processing file on the computer. She started it in 2000. I only skimmed the stuff but I made copies for both of you so you can look thoroughly."

We both got our laptops from our respective bedrooms and after grabbing a beer found comfortable places from which to work.

The file started as Irvin said about the time she got to college.

The first entry dealt with her impressions of the campus at the University of Pennsylvania, where she attended college. Her writing style was not very sophisticated. She didn't use a lot of colorful adjectives, just laid out the information in a straightforward manner without much youthful embellishment.

The first several pages went on in this vein, describing her professors, the people she met. She did make comments about the potential friends, more like notes to herself about how a possible friendship would work out. With the females she was more concerned with their sincerity and compatible interests.

With the males she addressed the possibilities of relationships and whether some might be a bit too sexually aggressive for her.

As the narrative went on the entries became more mature in tone. She had had her first sexual experience since leaving home in her sophomore year. She liked the partner all right but didn't see any chance of a long term relationship. He was simply too immature was the way she put it.

She talked some about her professors, the ones she liked and the ones she didn't like. She didn't just make statements but went on to chronicle the traits that she either liked or disliked about them.

She didn't appear to have many female friends. If she did she didn't talk about them much in the diary.

Sam took a break after about an hour. "You want another beer, either of you?" he asked.

Irvin said, "No, not right now thanks."

I said, "Yes, please."

The diary was more than 300 pages and Sam and I took our time reading it. We had no idea what we were looking for, but assumed that we would recognize anything significant.

Both of us took notes as we read the pages. Anytime she mentioned names we wrote them down on our notepads and the context of the item which mentioned them. It was tedious work and we only managed to get through about 100 pages before we decided to quit for the day.

"Let's go out for supper," I said.

James had been out most of the day looking at another security job for a business owner. He had just come in when I made the suggestion to go out for dinner.

"I'm up for that. I need to talk to you guys about the job I looked at today and that will be a good time to do it," he said.

We all climbed into my SUV and headed for the shopping mall, which had a couple of mediocre restaurants. The food wasn't bad and the prices were reasonable. We had agreed up front that each would pay his own bills in these situations so as to avoid hang-ups over whose turn it was to pay and such, unless one or the other volunteered up front to foot the bill.

The group was like brothers, except that I was the only white face in the group. We kidded around like siblings and none took offense at good natured ribbing. It was how I imagined life would have been with a brother or two in my family. I had a good deal of experience in interracial situations due to my football days, but our group was much closer than any of my football teams had ever been.

After we were seated and placed our orders I said to James, "Tell us about your day."

"We had an inquiry about some possible work that the guy didn't want to talk about over the phone. I arranged to meet him this morning, but not at his business address. We met at a McDonald's near where his store is located and he told me what it was all about."

"Why all the cloak and dagger?" Irvin asked.

"That was my first question to him," James continued. "He is missing money from the register but he doesn't know how much. The only way he determined that money was missing was by checking the inventory against his sales. The register scans all items sold by barcode. He knows how much of each product he orders and how much was sold over a given time. Using the wholesale price against the retail price he should come up with an exact figure for how much profit he realizes on each sale. The computer can then tell him what his profit should be for any given time frame. Do you understand what I am saying?"

Everyone nodded.

"Well, the numbers check out for sales, and the register tallies after each shift, but his profit margin is way down."

"Define way down," Irvin said.

"As much as $2,000 some weeks and always over a thousand a week."

"How could that be happening Irvin, if you can see a way?" I asked.

"I don't know. If the same number of items he bought equals the same number he sold, then there should not be any difference. If the register checks out at the change of shifts, then it's hard to see how any of the cashiers can be tapping the till."

"What kind of store is it?" I asked.

"A convenience store, like the one on almost every corner these days. Most are owned by immigrants from the Middle East, but this one is owned by a middle aged white guy. He's no dummy, but he is totally baffled by this. He wanted me to come up with some method to see what's going on."

"What about items like coffee and soda?" Sam asked.

"Possible I guess, but it would take a lot of those items to equate to the amount of money he says he is losing," Irvin said.

"So how are you going to solve this puzzle?" I asked.

"I can't. That's why I came to you guys. I don't even know where to start."

"I think the first step is to investigate the employees. Get their employment records and see how long each has been there. Then try to narrow down the time frame when he started to notice the cash missing. If you can get it down to one or two people then we can watch them and see if that leads anywhere. It's going to take a lot of man hours, so let him know up front that it won't be cheap," I said.

"Has he gone to the police with this?" Sam asked.

"No. He says he doesn't have anything to even show them what is missing, or even substantiate the cash as being stolen."

"He has a very good point. I'm not saying the police would laugh at him, but they certainly couldn't initiate an investigation based on what you have told us," I said.

"I don't even know how to estimate the number of man hours it would take to get a handle on the situation," James said.

"The employee check will be a piece of cake. We can get those from the police, or through Eddie Sanchez if necessary. Once the surveillance kicks in figure a week full time for two people. That's 80 man-hours times 50, that's four grand. Tell him we will look into it for a week for five grand, not guaranteeing anything. Tell him we will need a month's worth of his financial books to look at too. You can get Matt and Larry to do some surveillance. Irvin can look at the books and see if that tells us anything."

"I would feel better if you talked to him to explain the situation. I'm not sure he understands everything that we will be doing, since I don't understand what we hope to learn myself," James said.

I had to laugh at that. "I'm not sure I do either. What I suggested is just the most logical approach. If there are any accomplices we might be able to get a line on how it is being done. I will go with you to talk to him tomorrow if you set it up in the afternoon."

"Deal," James said.

Chapter 4

When we got up the next morning Sam and I started on the diary again.

It was still slow going but we were able to determine those with whom she maintained a continuing relationship throughout her college years. Nothing jumped out at either of us.

We broke for lunch and I went with James to meet the owner of the convenience store. We again met at McDonald's and I explained as best I could what I had in mind.

"We need to establish a suspect list, or at least narrow it down. All your employees are obviously suspects at this point, but we need to learn who the most likely culprit is. We might be able to determine that by observing lifestyle and associations. That's why I want a week to look at those currently employed."

"I would also like to have my financial expert look at a month's worth of your books. Would it be possible to get your financial data from the store for the previous month?"

"Sure. I have an accountant, but I keep my own books as well. I can provide you a copy of my files. Do you think anything will come of your efforts?"

"I can't make any promises, but someone who is stealing as much money as you say is missing will probably be living above their normal means. If that's the case it should show up in the things they purchase, how often they eat out, how expensively they dress, and other more subtle ways. It takes a very smart and cautious crook to put stolen money away without spending at least some of it. The background checks will tell us a lot about how the person should be living, and here I am talking about the type of housing and quality of the area in which they live. Like I said, there's no guarantees, but I feel we will at least be able to tell you who to keep a close eye on. We need a week and it will cost around $5,000."

"Then let's do that. How do I pay you?" he asked.

"I will have James bring you a contract spelling out the particulars, just so we both know what we are promising. We are going to need a list of all your employees. Can you point to some time frame when you started to notice the missing funds?"

"It has been going on for at least six months, I believe," he said.

They made arrangements for James to meet Mr. McCutcheon and get the list of employees the following day.

When they were on the way back home James said, "I really didn't think he would go for that."

"Why not. If he is losing $1,000 per week and it has been going on for six months he is out $26,000 already. If it continues he will certainly lose much more than what we are charging him. If we turn up anything it is money well spent. If we don't then he just adds our fee to his loss column," I said.

We had about four hours before we were supposed to meet at Lillian's house so Sam and I got back to the diary.

I had made it through her graduation and was mildly surprised that it continued with her trip to Europe. When I thought it through it made sense though. It was to be an exciting time and she would be experiencing new and different cultures, so in that light it made sense that she would want to capture those memories.

Her travels through England, Scotland, Germany and France were described with few references to specific people. She made a few comments about some good looking guy she had spotted on the tube, or near Buckingham Palace, but no specifics.

When she got to Cannes, France that changed.

She wrote that she had been near the waterfront when she noticed a good looking older man. By older she explained she meant in his early thirties to her estimation. She was intrigued enough to sort of follow along behind him until he went into a restaurant near the beach area. She was hungry and went in as well.

As it happened their tables were side by side and, both being alone, they struck up a conversation, which led to their both eating at her table.

She went on to say that his name was Omar Sharique. She thought it strange because it was so much like Omar Sharif, the actor, and commented on the similarity.

Omar, she said, was from Saudi Arabia and was somehow related to the royal family, at least according to him. She didn't totally discount the statement because he had his own yacht, though not a very large one. A yacht is still a yacht, she wrote.

They finished dinner and he asked if he might call her to have dinner on his yacht. She of course agreed and gave him the number of her hotel.

He had called the following day and even sent flowers to her room. He invited her for dinner that night and she accepted. He told her the name of the yacht and where it was berthed.

When she showed up he had champagne, and showed her around the boat. White jacketed waiters served the meal and they had two different kinds of wine with the meal. They moved to the deck and watched the traffic, both on the water and along the shore. More wine and she ended up spending the night on the yacht with him.

According to her diary he was nothing special in bed and struck her as somewhat chauvinistic. (How that came across from a roll in the hay I had no idea.)

Still, his boat, social status and charming manner kept her interested. He asked her to give up her hotel room and move onto the yacht with him but she refused. For some reason, she said, the image of white slavery popped into her head.

She slept with him three more times before he told her he was scheduled to move on to Portsmouth, in the United Kingdom to take care of some business. He was to leave the next afternoon.

They did not schedule anything for that night and she went to the same restaurant where they had first met. She spotted him going into the restaurant with another man. It dawned on her that she didn't even have a picture of him so she could brag to her closest friends.

She took her camera from her purse, waited for him to be seated, then went into the restaurant, snapping a picture of Omar and his friend, both of whom were in profile.

She then turned and left the restaurant.

This had all happened during late July of 2004. She checked out of the hotel the following morning and moved on to Rome and the remainder of her itinerary.

There was something about each of the places she visited but nothing about any other people.

I was intrigued by the man she called Omar. That was probably not his own name but one of convenience. I knew how the Middle Eastern mind worked, at least the male part of it. When they were away on 'business' trips, religion was not at the top of most of their priority lists. Omar seemed to be no different. If he was a devout Islamist there would have been no alcohol. The sex part he was not sure about whether the Koran prohibited it or not, though that was not germane to his investigation.

He made his notes and did not talk about the subject with Sam. He wanted to see what Sam's take was on the events in Cannes.

Sam had not finished before it was time to head to Lillian's, so he put his notes away and freshened up his appearance.

Sam washed his face and put on a more presentable pair of athletic shoes, which is all that I had ever seen him wear.

We headed to Burbank and got to Lillian's before Pamela arrived.

Lillian met us at the door. Merle was sitting in an easy chair watching the CNN news channel. He got up and shook our hands. "What are you into now?" he asked.

I gave him a brief synopsis and mentioned the similarity of the time element between this case and that of his wife that had brought us together.

"I haven't been able to find anyone who can shed light on any aspect of the case so far. Irvin got into her computer and we are digesting information from it."

The doorbell rang and I accompanied Lillian to the door. The young lady before us was around thirty, maybe five to ten pounds overweight, but with a clear complexion and very bright blue eyes. Her hair was blonde, though it might have been from a bottle. Still, I couldn't detect any darker roots. If it was dyed she had a very meticulous hairdresser.

I introduced myself and Lillian. As she walked through the door I added the names of Sam and Merle.

"I know of you," she said to Sam. "I'm a dyed in the wool UCLA fan and I remember your playing days."

"I'm honored," Sam said with a huge grin.

"Lillian is a psychologist, no longer practicing, and has some other talents that might possibly come into play. Merle you might also have heard of. He was once a pretty famous, or is it infamous, Hollywood producer," I said.

"I have heard of you, though if you asked me to quote one of your films I would have to disappoint you," Pamela said.

"Why don't you drop your purse on the coffee table and let's all sit around the dining room table. I have coffee on. There's some red or white wine, sodas, and even some lemonade," Lillian said.

Pamela turned back to me. "You look familiar but I can't place where I have seen you before."

Lillian bailed me out. "He is a private investigator, 'the private investigator' as a matter of fact who helped break up the smuggling ring recently. He, and Sam are also the ones recently in the paper for killing nine Mafiosi who tried to ambush them at his home. There was an interview on national news and a lot of play in the local papers."

"Oh yes. Now it comes back. I thought at the time how lucky you were to have escaped all that without serious injury," she said.

"We did have one man hurt, but not seriously. We had the advantage of knowing that they were coming and their intentions."

They continued to make small talk while Lillian served drinks. Pamela had a diet soft drink, while Sam and I had coffee. Lillian and Merle both had a glass of white wine.

Once we were all settled in I started the spiel. "As I told you on the phone, Carolyn's parents retained us to look into her disappearance. The police did not have any clues and Harry thought a fresh set of eyes might turn up some leads. We have been on the case for a couple of weeks and did manage to locate four folks who knew her and lived in the same apartment complex. All had nothing but good things to say about her. The picture we have come up with shows a well-rounded young professional woman who didn't seem to have many vices, and even fewer close friends."

"The last time she was seen, by anyone other than you, was Friday before she disappeared sometime that weekend." I stopped for breath.

"Does that make me a suspect?" Pamela asked, tongue in cheek.

We all got a laugh and I shook my head. "To the contrary, I am hoping you can tell me something of her state of mind that Saturday when you saw her. What was the circumstances, and what did you talk about that Saturday?" I asked.

"We had dinner at a restaurant north on 101 from her place. I can't remember the name of it, but it was a place we had gone before. I hate to inject my opinions into the narrative, but I have been giving the matter a lot of thought since your phone call and under the circumstances, I intuit that is exactly what you are looking for. Am I right?"

"Very much so. Anything that moves us further along the path to finding out what happened to her will be appreciated," I replied.

"Okay, she called me on Saturday morning and asked me if I wanted to meet her at her place and we would go out to dinner from there. That way we would only need one car. I agreed and we set the time for 6:00 pm. When I got there I didn't even go inside. She met me at the door and we went back to my car and I drove to the restaurant. She was somewhat quiet during the drive. She is not a very talkative person under normal circumstances, but that night she was quieter than usual. I remember feeling that she was thinking hard about something, but passed it off to our long relationship. You have to understand how close we were growing up. We were inseparable at school. We always tried to take the same classes and get the same teachers. I don't remember more than two or three classes all through high school that we didn't sit side by side, or front to back."

"We were both in class plays all the way through school. We fancied ourselves blooming actresses at the time. Anyway in retrospect I think she was unusually quiet that night. Something was bothering her, but she didn't bring it up. She didn't have much appetite and we ate in almost total silence. Finally I had enough and asked her what was eating at her."

"It's a personal problem," she said, "at least I think it is."

"You're going to have to explain that," I said.

"You remember the man I told you about meeting in Cannes?" she asked.

"Yes," I responded.

"It has to do with him."

"What about him?"

"I think he might not have been truthful with me when we were there."

"You mean he might have been married?"

She laughed. "That wouldn't make a lot of difference for such a short fling, would it?"

"Maybe not to some people, but it would to me," Pamela said.

"No. It's something else that I am not entirely sure about. It will take some time to sort it out," she said.

"She then changed the subject and the atmosphere lightened a bit for the remainder of the meal. On the way home she was more like her usual self. When we got back to her apartment I went in and we talked for a while, had a glass of wine and about 9:30 pm I left and went back to my place. That was the last time I saw her."

"Was the man she was referring to named Omar?" I asked.

"How did you know that?" she asked with astonishment.

"She wrote about it in a diary she left on her computer. She kept the diary throughout her college career and then for the graduation trip through Europe."

I looked at Sam. "I didn't want to get into this until you had time to go through it, but since it is on the table, she had an affair with an Arab yachtsman named Omar Sharique. She thought the name was cute because it reminded her of the actor, Omar Sharif. They were in Cannes and the affair only lasted about five days. I spent two years in the Middle East and I know the mindset. Arabic businessmen, when out of the country shuffle religion aside and become totally different people. Those who would die rather than drink alcohol in their native lands become falling down drunks in some cases. They carouse and sleep around, even the married ones, which I suspect was the case with Carolyn's friend Omar. What I don't know is what happened after Carolyn returned home. There's no mention of an address or telephone number in the diary, and no further entries about him after the Cannes incident."

"You think she might have kept in touch with him?" Pamela asked.

"I don't know, but from the tone of the diary I don't think she would have. She described him as chauvinistic. I suppose there was some glamor for a young woman, far from home and on her own, to find in a man apparently a seasoned traveler, probably very rich, and willing to lavish attention on her. It's something that bears looking into, but I am not sure I want to spring this on her parents at this stage of the game. If anything comes of it I might have to later, but for now I am inclined not to tell them."

"I agree with that," Pamela said. "It would hurt them unnecessarily and I don't see any point in doing that."

Everyone else at the table nodded agreement.

Lillian said, "Tell me everything you know about her."

"What kind of things do you want to know?"

"The mundane stuff. Was she religious? Did she have any phobias? Was she superstitious? Did she have a favorite place, a favorite dish, or even favorite clothing she wore until it fell apart? That kind of stuff."

"Why do you need to know those things?"

"I want to get the essence of her life. I am a psychic, though not a practicing one. I have been able to interface with the spirit world since childhood. It isn't something like my dialing the phone number of the spirit of someone and have them pick up on the other end. My encounters have all been initiated by the spirits, none of which I knew previously, except in the case of multiple contacts by the same spirit. Bradley was hoping that my sitting in might induce Carolyn to appear to me if there is something she wants to make known. Personally I place the odds of that happening very low, but it is possible."

"If it's a real séance' that you would like to see I will have to break out the props to get the setting right. In reality it makes no difference about props or even setting. When they are ready to appear it is just as likely to happen while I am watching television, or when I am trying to get to sleep," Lillian told her.

Pamela talked about Carolyn for almost an hour. Tears were in her eyes for a large part of the recitation. It was easy to see that the two young ladies were very close indeed.

In the end it was all educational but to no avail for spirit contact.

It was after 11:00 pm when they decided that nothing more could be accomplished and went their separate ways.

Chapter 5

On the way back to the house Sam asked me, "Do you think there might be a connection between her disappearance and this guy Omar?"

"It's a possibility we will need to look into, though I don't believe Omar Sharique is his real name. I also don't believe they kept in touch for nearly five years since the initial meeting. If that had been the case there would probably be more on the computer to indicate that. We need access to Carolyn's e-mail account to see if there has been any communication between the two," I said.

The next morning we called the Clayton's and went out to see them. I took along a contract spelling out our fee schedule and charged them $100 per man hour. I documented what we had done so far and the cost for that portion of the job. That alone came to almost $5,000.

Clayton wrote me a check for $5,000 and signed the contract.

"We managed to get onto her hard drive and are still working on the e-mail account. She didn't use any password reminders as some folks do, and it is a bit more difficult than my associate expected. We did get access to her word processing files and might have a tenuous connection from just after college. It's going to take some time to run that down."

"Pamela Whitehead was in her address book and we called her and talked face to face. She had dinner with Carolyn on the Saturday of that weekend. She thought that Carolyn was a bit withdrawn to the point that she asked her what was bugging her at dinner. Carolyn indicated that it was something of a personal nature and she seemed to perk up after that, according to Pamela."

"I know it doesn't sound like much, but it is progress. Now that we know that she might have been distraught about something it gives us a little better perspective for what we are dealing with."

"That is more progress than we have seen in five years, so keep plugging," Harry said.

"How much money do you want to put into this?" I asked.

"Let's call it $50,000 for now. If we reach that point we will revisit the situation."

"I can't promise to call every day, but I will make it a point to give you a verbal briefing at least weekly if that meets your approval. I am not much on paperwork unless it serves some concrete purpose. If you have questions, feel free to call me anytime," I said as Sam and I prepared to leave.

When we got back to the house Sam immediately got to work on the diary again, reading what I had discussed the previous evening at Lillian's.

After he finished he said to me, "I agree that he just picked her up for the sex. There would be no point in using his real name, and every reason to use an alias. I don't think he would bother to lie about his nationality. He would have no reason to. I think we can assume that he is a Saudi as a starting point, though that still leaves a few million suspects."

"It is possible that he told the truth about his connection to the royal family as well. That's a point of pride and might make him appear more desirable to a young lady such as Carolyn," I said.

"Okay, how do we identify him?"

"It's an almost impossible task based on what we have now."

We both went over the entry dealing with Cannes again, very carefully.

"We know the date so how about trying to get a list of the yachts moored in Cannes for that time frame?" Sam asked.

"It's a long shot, but worth a try. We will probably need to do it by mail, and it wouldn't hurt if we can get Eddie's department to make an official query. I will call him and see what he thinks."

I placed the call to Eddie's cellphone and explained the situation to him. "What do you think about an official query from the police department?"

"I believe you would be better served to go through the Westlake P.D. since you are working in their jurisdiction. I might be able to grease the skids for you. Let me make a call and I will get back to you."

He called back in less than fifteen minutes. "Go talk to the guy you saw before, Bill Hardwick. He says he will try to help. If you don't have any luck with that maybe your stock with the FBI is still high enough to get them to send an inquiry," he said.

I called Hardwick and set up an appointment for the following day.

When we arrived we were shown to his office.

I explained that we had a tenuous connection with someone in Cannes, France from 2005 and knew that the person in question owned a yacht that was moored there. We were trying to identify the person in question and if they had a list of the yachts in port then we could back track the owners and maybe shed some light on the person of interest. "What I want is an official request from the department asking if they still have records of the yachts in port during that specific week."

"I will have to clear it through my boss, but I believe he will go along if there's a possibility that it will shed some light on an unsolved case. Let me go ask him now, and if he agrees you can give me the dates while you are here. It will probably have to go out by mail."

"Whatever, as long as we get a response," I said.

Bill left us in his office and was back in less than five minutes. "He says go ahead and send the request by mail. I will ask that the response be marked for my attention and when I get it I will give you a call. Have you made any real progress?"

"We located a person who had dinner with her Saturday night, so whatever happened had to have happened between 10:00 pm Saturday and 7:00 pm Sunday."

"If you unearth anything else please let me know."

"We will do that, and when you get a response from Cannes, give me a call," I responded.

We had an early lunch and called Irvin to find out if he wanted some take-out. He did and we stopped for that.

I was at a loss as to what to do next. We needed some way to track the man she had met in Cannes. I mentally reviewed her diary entries and remembered she said she had snapped a photo of Omar and someone else in a restaurant. We had not looked at any of the pictures on the computer, and the chances that something from five years ago would be there were not really great, but it was another avenue we had not explored.

I asked Irvin about her picture files and he had a look.

"Wow, she must not have ever purged her files. There's over 2,000 pictures on here," he said.

"Can you copy the picture files and put them on a disc?"

"No sooner said than done."

A couple of minutes later he handed both Sam and me a copy of the file.

It appeared from the structure of the files that she had periodically downloaded the photos from her phone to the computer with nothing more than the date of the download. Fortunately her phone had a date time stamp on all the photos.

I cross referenced the diary entries to see if I could pinpoint the date she said she had taken the picture of Omar and his friend.

I got it close enough that I could identify the next download after that date and opened that file.

I found the picture I believe she was talking about and printed a couple of copies.

I handed one to Sam. "I think one of those two is Omar," I said.

"How does that help us?" he asked.

"I could send you to Riyadh with the picture and let you stand on the corner and compare everyone who passed to the photo," I said with a laugh.

"This boy ain't going to no place in the Middle East, at least until there is a bonafide reason to go," Sam said.

"Can't say that I blame you. It wasn't one of my favorite places either."

"How can we go about identifying these two guys? Correct me if I am wrong, but we don't even know which of the two we are interested in."

"I don't know. We will give it some thought. This at least gives us another avenue of approach."

"What if I try to get a directory of the Saudi royal family and see if they have pictures of them published? If they do I might be able to identify him that way," Sam said.

"It's worth a try. I will surf the web and look at articles involving the Saudi royal family and see if that yields anything," I said.

The two of us spent the remainder of the day on those chores without any luck.

Before we went to bed I told Sam and Irvin, "We have to come up with something that moves us along on the case and the only thing I can see that would do that is to identify one of the people in the photo."

"The government has some facial recognition software that I have heard is pretty good. If you can figure out who has it maybe you can get them to run the picture and see if anything pops up for them. I know they keep a vast data base on suspected terrorists, and the connection to the Middle East might be enough to get their interest," Irvin said.

"That's a good thought. I will do that first thing in the morning," I said.

After breakfast the next morning I called the San Francisco Special Agent in Charge of the FBI office. They had an office in L.A., but I had worked with him during the smuggling case and he seemed to be a pretty good guy. I was hoping that he could either tell who controlled the data base, or even better, have him submit the picture and ask for identification of the two parties.

When I told him what I wanted he asked, "What does the case concern?"

"A disappearance about five years ago in the Westlake area just north of Los Angeles. The police didn't turn up any clues and are treating it as a cold case. The parents hired me to look into it and I turned up a couple of things that the police had not picked up on. One thing was a contact by a friend on the Saturday night before her disappearance. Previously they had no known contact with her later than that Friday night."

"How does the picture come into the case?"

"I found a diary on her computer that she started in 2000. It carried right up through her graduation trip to Europe after graduation from college in 2004. She had a brief affair in Cannes, France with a man who owned a yacht and called himself Omar Sharique. The affair only lasted five days but she snapped a picture of him in a restaurant with another man the night before she left for the continuation of her trip. We haven't had any luck identifying the men in the photo."

"I can send it to Homeland Security and ask them to run it through their data base. If either of the two are there they should be able to identify them. I don't know for sure, but I think the CIA has a system that looks at all the facial features and tries to come up with a match. The problem is that if the men aren't in either of their data bases then it will be a meaningless effort."

"At least it will tell me if either of them are known," I said.

"Can you send me the photo in an email file?"

"I will do that today if you will give me the address to send it to," I said. "You can email me back the response if that is possible, or just call me and let me know what came of the effort. I really believe one of them, possibly both, were involved in her disappearance."

I terminated the call after writing down the e-mail address and told Irvin to send a copy of the photo to the address.

Chapter 6

James had gotten the list of employees from the convenience store owner and run record checks. Only minor stuff, like traffic violations, showed up on any of them. There were twelve in all and he had put Matt and Larry to work with the surveillance. They first located where each one lived and started separate folders on each of them.

They followed those on the day shift when they got off work. Each took a single individual and followed until they went home for the night, or until they discerned that it was not likely that they would be going out again before the next day.

Since they were not concerned with any rough stuff they shifted from one to another every couple of days.

Each kept copious notes on the activities of the targets, not knowing what might be useful.

With what had come in from the different jobs it seemed that they were at least making enough to justify their efforts.

It was the following Monday when I got the response back from the FBI. I got a call from the San Francisco SAC and he told me that someone from Homeland Security would be contacting me. Seems they had identified one of the people in the picture. They hadn't passed on much information, just the request for the meeting.

The call came later in the day. It was a man named Edward Slocomb. I invited him to the house and he showed up at 3:00 pm.

After the introductions he took the folder out.

"First of all, where did you get the picture?" he asked.

"Off the computer of the daughter of a client. She disappeared five years ago and we are trying to get a line on what possibly happened. The parents packed her computer up after the police finished their investigation and we retrieved if from their garage. The picture was taken by the missing daughter in Cannes, France in late June 2004."

"We got a hit on one of the people but it won't do you much good in your efforts I fear. It turned out to be one of the subway bombers from the attack in London in July of 2005. His name is Mahammad Sedique Khan. He died in the attack. The other man we didn't get anything on. Since the meeting took place long before the terrorist attack it could be that he is a player in some fashion. My boss wanted me to see if I could get enough follow-up information to try to run him down," he said.

"Since you have identified one of them that means that the other guy is the one we are looking for too. Also, since the terrorist attack in London took place in July of 2005 it means that he could not have been involved in the disappearance of the woman I am looking for," I said.

"What do you know about the other man?"

"He owns a yacht, probably a smaller one, and might be a Saudi Arabian. He was in Cannes, France during the last week of June, 2004, and we believe went from there to Portsmouth, England."

"What ties him to the woman you are investigating?" he asked.

"She kept a diary and the two of them had a brief fling in Cannes. To our knowledge she never heard from him after that. A close friend had dinner with her the night before she disappeared and recalled that her friend seemed distraught that night."

"Does the local police have this information?"

"No. I am working with the detective assigned to the case, but they didn't come up with any clues at all when they investigated the missing person report. I asked him to query Cannes to see if they had a list of yachts in port at the time in question. I didn't see the affair as pertinent to the case so didn't tell him about that. His department sent the request but we haven't heard anything back from them yet. I figured if we could nail down the name of the yacht we might be able to trace ownership and come up with an ID on the guy."

"When we got the hit on the terrorist we brainstormed a bit about the possibility that the other man in the picture could possibly be an accomplice, or at least someone who funds attacks of this nature."

"Do you have any technological ways to try to identify him that might not be available to me?" I asked.

"CIA has facial recognition software but I don't see how that would help at this point. If he had flown on a commercial airliner within the past couple of years our programs should have picked him up. Unfortunately we only have photographs from U.S. carriers. If he is from the Middle East, which you seem to have confirmed, then we are fighting an uphill battle trying to identify him," Edward said.

"Is the fact that he met with a suicide bomber just a year before the terrorist act significant enough for you guys to try to help me get a line on him?" I asked.

"Definitely, but don't expect much in the way of information that will help with your case. We will add his picture to the list of persons of interest and see if anything surfaces. If he is supporting terrorists he will be keeping a low profile," Edward said.

He gave me one of his business cards and I returned the favor. "Please let me know if you find out anything at all," I said as I walked with him to the door.

Neither Sam nor Irvin, the only others in the house at the time, had contributed anything.

"What do you guys think?" I asked after Edward left.

"At least we know which guy we are interested in now," Sam said.

"There's that, but I wish they would have come up with more," I said.

"Don't give up yet. The query about the yachts might turn up something," Irvin, ever the optimist, said.

"We're stuck unless we come up with other clues," I said.

"I'm still trying to get into her e-mail account. Maybe I will have some luck with that sooner or later," Irvin said.

I had not been in touch with Lillian for several days and was thinking about bringing her up to date. I called and asked her if she and Merle wanted some take-out food and company for dinner.

"Sure, get chicken. I never tire of that. Who's coming with you?"

"Just Sam."

"See you when you get here," she said and hung up.

I took a copy of the picture with me to Lillian's.

We got the chicken at KFC and when we arrived Lillian had the table set for four. I handed her a copy of the picture. She took one look and said, "That looks like one of the subway bombers from the London attack."

"Well, so much for my intention of impressing you with what we have learned," I said.

Sam almost fell out of his chair laughing.

"Where did the picture come from?"

"From Carolyn's computer. She took it the night before she left Cannes. The other one is the one she had a brief affair with," I said.

"Remember Pamela said Carolyn was somewhat out of sorts the night they had dinner? What if she was looking at her pictures and made the connection I just made?" Lillian asked.

"I suppose that's possible, but what could she have possibly done about it?" I asked.

"That's the big question, and unfortunately, I haven't the slightest idea."

"Still, that opens a different line of approach. If she tried to contact the other man in the photo that could have led to her disappearance. I haven't tried to check her cell phone records, and Irvin still hasn't gotten into her computer e-mail files."

Merle asked, "Can you go to her cellular company and get the files from the date in question?"

"I don't think I can, but the police might be able to, assuming cellular companies keep records that far back," I replied.

"Are your clients satisfied with the progress you've made?" Merle asked.

"They seem to be. I had a meeting with them and passed on what I have learned, minus their daughter's affair part of it. I asked him how far he wanted to go and he said $50,000 and we would re-evaluate based on what progress had been made. He's a lot like you were Merle. He just wants some closure and if we can identify someone who did her harm he wants them to pay for it," I said.

"I can certainly understand where he is coming from, though I had a bit more prodding than he and his wife have had."

"They're fairly wealthy and I can understand their actions. If I had a missing daughter under the same circumstances I think I would be just like them."

"Even if you can identify and locate the other man in the photo you still have to prove that he was involved," Lillian added.

"Yes, but knowing his identity should open some other approaches to that part of the problem. The Department of Homeland Security has placed his photo on their list of persons of interest. If they get any results from that it might help. I still believe that whatever we need to help solve the case is on Carolyn's computer, specifically in her e-mail files. Irvin has been working on that since we discovered the computer without any positive results."

"He's very tenacious," Lillian said, "He will solve the problem sooner or later."

"I sure hope it is sooner. I don't know where to turn right now, unless the query to Cannes about the yachts reveals something we can use," I said.

We talked through the meal and dessert that Lillian had prepared. It was after 9:00 pm when Sam and I left.

On the way back to our place Sam asked what I planned to do about the cell phone angle.

"I suppose we can get in touch with her cellular company and see if they have any records back that far. Just learning if they do will help us to see what calls she made and received that Saturday night and Sunday. I believe we can talk the Westlake PD into requesting the information if it's available," I said.

"And what if that doesn't work?" Sam asked.

"Then I guess we are back to square one, the computer. We really need to get access to her e-mail file."

I checked with Irvin when we got back home. He was still hunched over the computer but I could tell by his posture that he was still searching for something he had not been able to find.

Sam and I said good night and went to our respective bedrooms.

Chapter 7

I always place my cell phone on the bedside table before I go to bed and had done so on that night.

When I heard the ring tone I glanced at the clock. It was 3:18 am. I wondered who could be calling at that hour as I reached for the phone. I glanced at the caller ID and found that it was Lillian.

"Okay, what's so urgent at 3:18 in the morning?" I asked by way of greeting.

"I had a vision that you need to know about," she said.

"Well don't keep me in suspense," I replied.

"Carolyn appeared to me in a dream. I know that sounds like one of the biblical prophets starting to tell of a visit from God, but I don't know how else to describe it. I know I was asleep when it happened, but I don't know at what point it happened. It could have been right after I fell asleep or just before I awoke, but I remember it clearly. It was Carolyn and she seemed to materialize from nowhere and said, ambrosia 13. She seemed to hesitate and then said, Ellen Norton. I have no idea what either of those two statements mean but figured you could puzzle it out," she said.

"Hold on and let me get a pencil."

I rummaged through the drawer of the nightstand until I found a pen and told her to repeat them.

"Ambrosia 13 and Ellen Norton," she said.

I wrote them down. "That was all? She didn't give you any indication as to what they meant?"

"That's it. If it had happened while I was awake I might have been able to question her and find out the context, but that's all there was to it. It couldn't have taken more than a few seconds, then she just disappeared."

"I will check them out later this morning and see if I can make sense of them, and thank you for calling."

After we hung up I had a tough time getting back to sleep. I thought about the two things Lillian had told me. Ellen Norton was obviously a name, though I didn't know anyone by that name. The other part of the message didn't ring any bells. I knew that ambrosia was a dish featuring a variety of fruits, but that didn't make any sense to me.

I tossed and turned for perhaps an hour and was just at the point of falling asleep again when my mental alarm bells started ringing. What if Ambrosia 13 was the password to Carolyn's e-mail account! I couldn't wait until daylight. I pulled on a pair of trousers and went to Irvin's room. I knocked, none too lightly, and pushed the door open. Irvin was stirring and I said, "Get up and put on a pair of pants. I have something I want you to try." I then closed the door and went to the kitchen to put the coffee on.

A couple of minutes later when Irvin came out, still half asleep, he said, "It's the middle of the night and I don't think we are being attacked, so what's so important that it has to be done right now?"

I pointed to the Carolyn's computer and said, "Fire that thing up."

Irvin moved to the computer and turned it on.

I went back to the kitchen and got us each a half cup of coffee by removing the pot and allowing the brewed stuff to drip right into the cups.

"Okay, what now?" he asked.

"Try ambrosia 13 for the e-mail password," I said.

He navigated to the e-mail server and entered the password I had supplied. The computer wouldn't allow him to access the web site but the deleted e-mails and the ones she sent showed up on the menu.

"Bingo!" he cried loud enough to awaken Sam, who came staggering into the room still half asleep.

"What's going on?" he growled.

"We got into Carolyn's e-mail," Irvin said.

"How did you come up with the password?" Irvin asked.

"I got a call from Lillian a few minutes ago and she told me she had a dream in which Carolyn appeared and gave it to her, though she didn't say what it meant. She just said ambrosia 13, then she said, Ellen Norton. The latter is obviously a name but I don't know anyone by that name," I said.

"What was the name again?" Sam asked, coming awake a bit more.

"Ellen Norton," I said.

"I think that is the name of one of the employees of the convenience store case that James is working on," he said.

"I know James has not been asleep long but roust him out."

I went back to the kitchen and refilled my cup and Irvin's. I also poured a cup for James and Sam. We all met in the kitchen once James was up.

"Carolyn's spirit appeared to Lillian sometime during the night. She called me at 3:18 am to tell me. She gave us the password for the e-mail, and apparently the name of the person who has been stealing from the convenience store," I said.

"How could she even know about the convenience store case?" James asked.

"I have no idea. She didn't elaborate on either of the phrases and Lillian had no idea what she was talking about. She only appeared for a matter of seconds according to Lillian."

"When I ran the name, which is Ellen Norton, by Sam he seemed to think that was the name of one of the store employees. Is that the case?"

"It sure is. This is absolutely amazing," James said.

"So what does this tell us?" James asked.

"Number one, that you now know who to concentrate on to solve the case of the missing money at the store, and that Carolyn is indeed dead. I held out hope that she might still be alive, but I think this confirms that she is in fact dead," I said.

"It also means that she wants to make sure we catch her killer," Sam offered.

"Now that we know we can get into the e-mail, let's go finish our naps. I have a feeling today is going to be a long one," Irvin said as he set his half-finished coffee in the sink and headed back to bed.

We all did the same and managed to sleep for a couple of more hours. I was so excited that I could hardly sleep. I must have slept for 30 minutes during the two hours I lay in bed.

James agreed to fix breakfast after we were all up. He is not the world's greatest cook, but no one else wanted the chore and allowed him to do it. He had a bowl of cereal, or rather a bowl for the cereal, plus boxes of the stuff set out on the table. He had fixed two pieces of toast each and set the milk, coffee pot and condiments on the table.

Let me tell you it was one of the quickest breakfasts any of us had eaten in quite some time. We were all as anxious as a high school debutante waiting for her first date to pick her up.

Five minutes maximum it took us to scarf down the cereal and toast. We all followed Irvin to the computer and dragged up chairs.

Irvin first navigated to her e-mail address book and printed copies for all of us. "You guys be looking at those while the maestro goes to work. I hate having you breathing down my neck."

We each took our copy of the e-mail address book and started to look at it from our own prospective. I first compared it to the regular address book we had earlier gotten from the computer. I quickly eliminated those for whom we had other contact information and started looking at what was left.

Her e-mail list was quite lengthy and even after eliminating the names we had run across before the list still contained more than 30 names. The first one I searched for was Omar Sharique, the man she had the affair with in Cannes. Much to my disappointment he wasn't on the list.

I next tried to determine if any on the list were foreigners. That also drew a blank. I was now sure that somehow the e-mail file was the key, otherwise Carolyn would not have appeared to Lillian and given her the password for the program.

I spent two hours with the list and was no closer to finding anything usable than when I started. I asked Sam and James how they were faring and found they were in the same boat as I was.

Irvin had been going through her sent message file and had not indicated anything to the rest of us, either positive or negative.

I was going to need to look at what Irvin was now looking at in order to make any progress, and even then I would have to come across something that would lead us forward on the case.

When we broke for lunch James said, "I want to get Matt and Larry both on the woman whose name Lillian gave you. I still don't understand how Lillian could be associated with that, but since I met you all kinds of screwy things have happened, so I will concentrate on her."

"It might have been that she knew about what we were working on and wanted to help us get that out of the way so we could concentrate on her case," I said.

"You really think so?" James asked.

"I don't know, but that makes sense. I don't have the foggiest idea about how dead people go about finding out things, I just know that my experience tells me that they don't send us off on wild goose chases. Carolyn provided the name, so I have to believe that she is the guilty party. Now all you need to do is figure out how she is doing it and catch her in the act. You might not even need to catch her. If the store owner is confident that she is the guilty party he can just fire her and the thievery will stop. On the other hand he will need a reason to fire her or the labor people will be down on him like birds on bread crumbs," I said.

"Are you still going to try to get the phone records for her cell phone?" Sam asked.

"Yes, I am," I said.

I called Harry Clayton right then and asked him if he knew what company Carolyn used for her cell phone. The answer was Sprint.

I next called Sprint, and after going through several layers of programmed responses, finally got a live person on the line. When I explained what I wanted she said she had no idea if they kept records that long, or who I would need to talk to about the subject.

I bit my tongue and thanked her.

"Looks like I am going to have to make a trip to the Sprint store to see about that," I said.

I wanted to get out of the house, so I asked Sam if he wanted to take a ride to the shopping mall.

There was a Sprint kiosk there but they didn't have full service. You could purchase a phone, have it activated, or make changes to your contract, but the young man could not answer my questions. I asked where the nearest full service store was located and got the address.

We had better luck there. I was told that it might be possible to get a list of the phone's activity for a given time frame, but the request would have to be made by the next of kin in the case of someone deceased.

"What about a request from a law enforcement agency?" I asked.

"I don't know how they handle those, but I am sure they will be provided."

As I talked to the customer representative it suddenly dawned on me what an idiot I had been. I turned to Sam.

"We didn't even check her phone," I said.

"That's because we don't have her phone to check. It disappeared along with her," he said.

I know I must have looked like a child who had lost his favorite toy, and my voice must have betrayed that feeling, because Sam said, "Just because you're the boss doesn't mean you don't have mental lapses occasionally."

"I am adequately chastised," I said.

"Let's go talk to Bill Hardwick and see what he recommends," Sam suggested.

We drove to the police building in Westlake, only to find that Bill was out of the office.

Since administrative people usually know more about the kind of thing I was interested in I took a chance and asked the clerk if she had any idea about how to acquire a list of phone calls made from a cell phone.

"If you know the number and the service provider it's just a matter of sending them a request for the numbers of all calls sent and received during a specified time frame."

"Do you know if they will provide the data to a private investigative firm?"

"I don't believe they will. There's too much chance they will get burned for unauthorized disclosure."

"Thank you. You have been very helpful. Could you ask Bill to call me when he gets back to the office?"

"I will leave a message on his phone," she replied.

As we left the police station I said to Sam, "Let's stop by and see Lillian. It was the wee hours of the morning when she called and I want to be sure she told me everything that happened with Carolyn."

Sam called her as I got on the freeway heading south.

"Hey sweet thing," Sam said. "Me and Brad are on the way over. You going to be home?"

"Let me check my social schedule." She paused momentarily. "I think I can fit you in. Come on over."

"I love that lady's sense of humor," Sam said after he hung up.

"She is still pretty feisty for her age," I replied.

We were there within half an hour.

We sat at the table with Lillian and Merle.

"The name you gave me in the wee hours this morning was one of the employees of a convenience store we are investigating. The owner has been losing over $1,000 per week and can't figure out how he is being bilked. He hired us to look into the matter. When we connected the name we assumed that she was giving us information about the other case. Can you see any other reason for the name coming up during her visit?" I asked.

"No. If you know the name then she is obviously trying to help you solve another case. For what reason I haven't the slightest idea. It is out of the norm, and could be like Merle's wife appearing and asking me to put the advertisement in the paper for the express purpose of getting you to contact me. I only know that the spirits never provide bad information. By that I mean that everything they have provided to me in the past has been directly related to something that concerns them. I don't know how Ellen Norton fits into your affairs, but she definitely plays some part."

"Do you think it might go beyond just helping us solve another case?"

"As I said, I really don't know anything for sure, but if I were a betting person I would bet that she is in some way involved with the case related to Carolyn. It just doesn't feel right for her to provide the name unless that is the case."

"Boy, that's another curveball," Sam said.

"I suppose we will have to dig up all we can on her past to see if we can find some connection to Carolyn before her death. I have a list of everyone in Carolyn's e-mail address book and I have gone over it at least twice. I don't remember that name being on the list," I said.

"Nor do I, and I have gone over it at least three times," Sam added.

"I don't know what to tell you. I am just the conduit," Lillian said.

"You said you didn't know exactly when she appeared to you, but that you were asleep when it occurred," I said trying to lead Lillian into some memories that might shed more light on the appearance.

"I went to sleep around 11:00. I called you at 3:18. It happened somewhere in that time frame but I don't know when. I just know that when I awoke it was at the forefront of my consciousness."

"What connection could a convenience store clerk have with someone of Carolyn's stature?" I asked, more or less thinking out loud.

"You're the detective," Lillian said. "You will have to figure that out. But when you do, don't forget to tell me about it."

On that note, Sam and I headed back home.

Chapter 8

Sam and I were both pensive on the drive back to the house. I was mentally trying to look for any possible way Carolyn could be connected to Ellen Norton. It just didn't make sense to me.

Sam was apparently in the same boat, and mood, because he didn't say more than half a dozen words all the way back home.

When we walked in Irvin said, "I have printed out all the messages she sent and received from the weekend before her disappearance. Nothing jumped out and bit me, but maybe you will have better luck."

I looked at the stack of messages Irvin had printed. Instead of printing multiple messages on a single page he had only put one message per page and included the address data with each one.

James was still out with Larry and Matt.

I was still bogged down by what possible part Ellen Norton could play in the disappearance of Carolyn Clayton. I simply was not in the mood to go through the messages and said so. "I'm going to get a beer and relax for the remainder of this miserable day."

"Does that include the hired help?" Sam asked.

"Yes, and that includes you Irvin. You need to take a break. You have been on that computer for weeks."

"I kick back while you guys are gone. I only move back to the computer when I hear the car pull up," he said.

We knew he was pulling our chain because of the amount of data he provided to us. He could not do that without putting in an awful lot of hours.

"Just the same, grab a beer and let's hit the patio."

As we sat around the patio drinking the beer I told Irvin about the last conversation with Lillian. "She seems to believe that the spirit providing the name means that she is involved in the main case. She has enough experience in that area to have a better feel for the situation than any of us do. Although it seems very unlikely to me that the two will tie together in some way, I trust Lillian's instincts more than my own."

"The logic seems to fit. If she has never encountered any spirt that gave her extraneous information there's no reason for this case to be any different," Irvin said.

"You guys are way over my head with all this philosophical discussion. I'm going for another beer. Anyone else ready?"

I shook my can to see how much was left and nodded affirmative. Irvin said he was okay.

We whiled away the early evening hours playing 'what if' based on what we knew and what we could deduce from what we knew.

It had gotten dark and we had consumed three beers each. I had not heard back from Bill Hardwick and figured he would call first thing in the morning. I was getting heavy eyelids and none of us had eaten supper yet.

"You guys want to go out for supper?" I asked.

Sam agreed, but Irvin wanted to work some more. "I will grab a sandwich," he said.

James had not shown up all day and I called him.

"You want to meet us for supper?" I asked when he picked up.

"No. We grabbed a burger a bit ago. I am with Larry and Matt. We are watching Ellen Norton's house."

"Okay. Talk to you in the morning," I said and disconnected the call.

Sam and I had supper and returned to the house.

We both went to bed early.

The following morning we all went to Denny's for breakfast. James said, "I don't know what to make of Ellen Norton. She lives in a pretty decent neighborhood and seems to live alone. We have not observed any male visitors, nor any children. She seems to be on the permanent day shift and it would make it more difficult for her to be doing what we suspect she is doing while the store is at its busiest."

"The three of us were rehashing the situation and decided that she might be tied in with Carolyn Clayton in some way.

Lillian says that none of her contacts with the departed have resulted in information about anything other than the actual person in question. We decided that it is possible that she fits into Carolyn's disappearance in some way."

"Boy, that's really a stretch," James said. "They certainly wouldn't tend to belong to the same social circles."

"At any rate I am going to try to find a connection. She's not in Carolyn's regular address book or her e-mail file, so the relationship would not have been very close, at least not within the few years before Carolyn disappeared," I said.

Irvin said, "I can google her when we get back to the house. That might turn up something."

"You don't think she is the thief?" I asked James.

"We certainly have better candidates. One of the night people is a younger guy and he seems to go out a lot more than one would think from the salary he makes, which can't be more than $15 or so per hour. Even with a shift differential he wouldn't be making more than 40 K annually. He habitually sleeps about six hours after his shift and then is up and out of the apartment. Sometimes he doesn't go back until just before his shift is to start. We have followed him to bars, video game parlors, and to the beach. We haven't been inside the bars to see how heavily he drinks, but you can bet that he spends more than he makes at the lousy job he has. The apartment rent has to be between $1,000 and $1500 per month. Add the utilities and he isn't going to have much left to live on."

"What's his name?"

"Trevor Whitmore."

"What did his rap sheet look like?"

"Two traffic violations are all that showed," James said.

"You feel he is a much better suspect than Ellen?" I asked.

"Definitely. He is under 25 years old and his lifestyle seems to fit better."

"Okay, concentrate on him and see if you can get into one of the bars he frequents. Look for any one he meets regularly and see if you can get an idea of the kind of money he is spending."

"What are you going to do about Ellen?"

"Try to find out if she possibly knew Carolyn Clayton."

"How are you going to go about that?"

"My first stab at it will be to call Pamela Whitehead and see if the name might ring a bell for her. Ellen and Carolyn would be roughly the same age and it is possible that they knew each other sometime in the past," I said.

I asked James to drive us back home and got on my phone. I didn't like bothering Pamela at work but called anyway.

When she answered I identified myself and asked her if the name Ellen Norton meant anything to her.

She gave the matter some thought. "There was a girl by that name in our high school class. I don't remember much about her, except the name. She was somewhat withdrawn and didn't have many friends as I recall. Why are you interested in her?"

"Lillian had a dream and her name came up," I said.

"Really! I don't believe in that stuff, but she would have to do a lot of research to come up with that name out of the blue."

"Now that the connection is established it makes more sense," I said. "I will call you later and bring you up to date."

"Now that you know there's a connection you have to figure out what it means," Sam said.

"You mean, we have to figure out what it is," I said.

"This is starting to get really complicated."

"Yes, but the more pieces of the puzzle we find the more sense it will make."

Irvin did the search on Ellen Norton when we got back to the house. He turned up more than the police report showed and went to one of the sites that provides all known information on a person, for a small fee of course.

When he got the address of the family during her childhood I looked at a map and found that it was in the same area for the high school that Carolyn and Pamela had attended, so that part checked out.

Irvin also found that she had an arrest for possession of controlled substances, read dope, in 2003. The case was either dropped or they got her into a rehab program.

"What do you guys think? Do we have enough to confront her and try to find out what she knows about Carolyn's disappearance, or do we dig more first?"

"I believe we want to talk face to face with Pamela, and probably in the presence of Lillian, but I don't know if we should wait or go with what we have now," Sam said.

Irvin said, "I can access her yearbook and see if that helps any. Sometimes people put weird things in those. It will give us a better idea about how she was perceived by her peers, and might lead us to other associations that are important if she is involved."

"Then you have the rest of the day. Tomorrow I will visit the convenience store, just before the shift changes, and try to talk to her. Since I can have some names from her yearbook it might help to convince her to talk to me," I said. "I will call Lillian and set up a meeting. I know she will be interested to know how the name fits into our puzzle. It is possible that the additional knowledge will entice the spirit of Carolyn to contact her again, though that is what the bookies call a long-shot."

Bill Hardwick called and I asked him if he could request the list of calls from Sprint.

"What's the purpose?" he asked.

"I want to see who she spoke with from Saturday morning until she disappeared. It might give us another clue," I said.

"Give me the number and carrier."

I provided the information he asked for and he said he would get back to me either later in the day or the following day.

Sam, Irvin and I were back at Lillian's that evening. We again got food along the way, this time Chinese.

Once the conversation started I told Lillian, "I think you were right about Ellen Norton being tied to Carolyn's disappearance. They went to the same high school. While Ellen works at the convenience store we are surveilling, it looks like we have a better candidate as the thief."

"What did you find out about her that might help with the case?" Lillian asked.

John Buckner

"She had an arrest for possession of narcotics in 2003 but it never went to trial. I imagine she got into some sort of treatment program or half way house. The police aren't nearly as interested in prosecuting users as they are dealers. It could also be that she gave up the name or names of her supplier(s)."

"How is that going to help?" Lillian asked.

"I don't know. It's just another thing to look into. What we are really trying to do is establish a connection between her and Carolyn since high school. Pamela remembered her from school but said that she was unremarkable. She apparently didn't run with the same crowd," I responded.

"Deep down you believe she knows something that will help you solve the case, don't you?" Lillian asked.

"I guess in a way I do. Like you, I don't think Carolyn's spirit would have given you the name unless it meant something."

"Well the one thing you can be sure of is that Carolyn is indeed dead, otherwise her spirit would not have appeared to me," Lillian said.

"Believe it or not I had figured that out on my own," I said, then apologized for the remark. Lillian was just trying to make sure I was aware of all the facts.

"This case is becoming more complicated with each passing day," she said.

"Tell me about it. I need to find out what part Ellen plays in this in the worst way," I said.

"When are you going to talk to her?" Lillian asked.

"Tomorrow after she gets off work unless Irvin can come up with additional information between now and then," I said.

"You still think there is a tie in to Omar?"

"It would seem the most logical explanation. There's no proof, but the diary and picture sure point in that direction."

"Correct me if I am wrong, but you didn't find anything more about Omar on her e-mails?"

"No, no contact with him that was obvious. I haven't gone through all the e-mails yet, but he is definitely not in her address book."

"Then I believe that Ellen is connected in some way that isn't obvious. Remember the password and the name were provided at the same time. We just assumed that Omar was the reason for the spirit to appear," Lillian explained further.

"That's true. We might have been barking up the wrong tree from the start."

"All the evidence pointing to him is circumstantial at best," Lillian said. "What if he is not a player at all?"

"Then we are back to looking for a motive, and even more important, someone else who would have had a reason to kill Carolyn," I said.

"I think that's where you are. I believe Omar was probably tied to the London attacks in 2005, but that doesn't help with your case. On the other hand you may have helped to root out another terrorist money-man," she said. "Sometimes the government offers rewards for information leading to such people. You have established that he knew one of the bombers and if you can get an identity Uncle Sam might be quite generous."

"I hadn't thought about that angle. I might shake the bushes a bit and see how interested old Uncle Sam really is."

When we left Lillian's I think we were all giving serious thought to her comments. I kept forgetting how sharp she is.

"What do you guys think about changing our focus to Ellen?" I asked.

"What Miss Lillian said made a lot of sense," Irvin said. "She is really sharp for her age."

"I think that means we want to reestablish surveillance on her, especially after I have a talk with her tomorrow."

"I'll have Matt switch back to watching her in the evening and early nighttime hours," James said.

The rest of the way home we bantered about how Ellen could possibly be connected but came to no conclusions.

Chapter 9

Bill Hardwick called me the following morning. "We have heard back from Cannes. They did have the list in their computer files and sent it. I will make a copy for you and you can stop by and pick it up. I also have the list of calls made from the phone number you gave me. I added a couple of days on the front end just to be on the safe side. What kind of progress are you making on the missing person case?"

"Some, but not enough to get your interest yet. The phone logs might shed some more light on where we think this is going but we won't know for a while," I said.

"Well, they're here when you can find time to pick them up. If I have to be out of the office I will leave them with the receptionist," he said.

I was anxious to see what was in both files and grabbed Sam and hit the road to Westlake. It was after 10:00 when we got there, having stopped for a quick breakfast along the way.

Bill was not in the office and I got the lists from the receptionist in a plain white envelope with my name written on it. I let Sam drive so I could look the lists over while we were on the way back home.

The phone log only had numbers listed, no names. That would be a job for Irvin, running down the identities associated with each of the numbers.

The list from Cannes was a bit more voluminous than I thought it would be. Since it is a relatively small port I figured there would be 20 to 30 yachts there at a time. There were over 100 on the list. I didn't think they had that much pier space and surmised that they were including the ones anchored out, as we used to say in the military. I wasn't sure about the dates of the film festival held there and that could be another factor which drove the numbers up.

Each yacht had a registration number and a name. No other personal information was included. I figured I could run the names through the registration data base the Maritime agency kept and eliminate many of them pretty quickly.

I had no idea how Irvin would handle the list of phone numbers. I knew that there was a reverse look-up feature on the internet, for a small fee, of course, but I didn't know if they kept archived numbers.

I voiced my thoughts to Sam as we tooled along the freeway.

How inconsiderate of Carolyn not to have taken a picture of the yacht. That would certainly make the job of identifying Omar's boat a lot easier. As it stood we could probably eliminate all those owned by non-Arabs, but that was still going to leave a lot to look into, I thought. I wanted to get a definite identity of the boat and then follow that to a name so I could have some bargaining chips when I talked to the government again about the possible terrorist tie-in.

The government had the same information we did, that is, the picture, place and date. If they were not able to connect the same dots we had and I should come up with the name I could provide it to them, then that would give me some legal claim to a reward, if one was offered.

I was putting the cart before the horse in this case but I am after all, an optimist.

When we arrived back at the house I passed the list of phone numbers to Irvin and sat at my own computer and started working on the ship files. I went to the International Ship's Registry site and one by one I fed the yacht names into the system and made a list of the ones registered in Arabic countries. The list of 104 shrunk to 12 just that easily. I next extracted the ones registered in Saudi Arabia. That list had three names.

I then went to a different web site to see if I could access the Saudi Arabia Maritime agency to find out who owned the three yachts. Just like that I had the names. Now all I had to do was decide which of the three was our boy.

I asked Irvin to see what he could find out about each of them.

He suspended the number search and googled the three names from my list. All were connected to the house of Saud in some way. And our luck was still holding because there were pictures of all three. Irvin printed the files and then copied them to a picture file. From there he accessed the file and extracted the pictures. He blew them up and enhanced the quality. All were bearded but I thought I could recognize Omar, even with the beard. Sam and Irvin agreed with my choice.

I had Irvin print just the picture of the man we knew as Omar, but whose real name was Abdul Fahad Sarraf. According to what we could find out about him, he was a distant member of the royal family of Saudi Arabia, or the House of Saud. With the name we were able to do further research and build a profile of him.

He was wealthy, as were most of the royal family, and did most of his travelling on his yacht. Occupation wise he was in the oil business (what else) and dabbled in stocks. His home was his office, which could be translated to mean he didn't work at all, though he would have to make some decisions about his oil business. Like a lot of others he probably had a Texan running the effort.

Nowhere in Carolyn's diary did she give a good description of her 'Omar'. She had not indicated if he had a beard or was clean shaven, or if he dressed in robes or business suits. The picture she took showed him in a business suit with a beard, though not as full as most mature Arabs wore.

I built a dossier on him, combining all the information we had and added some suppositions, such as the fact that he might have been headed for Portsmouth, England when he left Cannes. This would indicate that he could have had further contact with Mohammad Siddique Khan, or any of his accomplices.

Suicide bombers don't usually take the big step until they are assured that their relatives will be cared for in some way. Since the date of the meeting in Cannes was a year earlier than the attacks one might assume that Sarraf was making assurances that all would be well for those left behind.

I personally would never go for the delayed payment option if I were about to embark on a suicide mission. I would insist on cash up front and in the bank before I strapped on explosives. I could never see myself doing that, even if the reward was in fact

100 virgins. Who's to say that you will still be able to enjoy sex after death anyway?

Procreation certainly isn't mentioned in the Bible in any of the descriptions I have read about how things are to be. Maybe Muslims go to a different heaven!

Anyway I tried to follow my old procedures for putting together reports for the government. It doesn't matter what part of the bureaucracy you occupy, the procedures are the same.

When I finished I printed two copies and handed one to Sam and one to Irvin. "Read that and tell me what you think," I said.

Both read it rather quickly, not taking what I thought was adequate time to savor the words I had labored over for the better part of two hours.

"Looks good to me. I think you hit all the key points and the photograph is the clincher. It clearly shows him with the London Bomber and the photo is date/time stamped, which I suppose could be added after the fact for those conversant enough with photo shop," he said.

"I think it is enough to establish the fact that we have identified a potential terrorist for certain. If that's the only criteria then we are in business," Irvin added.

"I have to get this to Homeland Security, but I don't want to go through Edward Slocomb, though I have no axe to grind with him. He knows enough that he might try to shift the glory to his own shoulders, as a lot of bureaucrats do. I think I will send this to the queen's palace, since it does, after all, resemble the Holy Grail, metaphorically speaking," I said.

"Even if you send it to her there's no guarantee that she will see it as coming from you. Someone in the queen's chambers might want to take the credit," Irvin said.

"I can send it registered, return receipt requested. That way I will know who signed for it," I said.

"Also," I continued, "I am going to identify where and who generated it within the correspondence." When I finished the letter it looked like this:

From: Bradley Kinkaid
       Kinkaid Investigations
       Prescott, Arizona
To: Director of Homeland Security
Subj: Possible terrorist link: Abdul Fahad Sarraf

While investigating a case for a private client, I and my associates uncovered information that leads me to believe the subject of this letter has ties to terrorists.
He was seen in Cannes, France in the company of one of the London subway bombers, Mohammad Sedique Khan. The person in question is Abdul Fahad Sarraf and he is a Saudi Arabian.
The enclosed picture was taken in late June of 2004, as you can see from the time stamp, in Cannes. Sarraf then went by private yacht to Portsmouth, England.
I suspect that he might be the money behind that and other terrorist acts. I do not have the time and resources to pursue the matter privately.
If there is a reward for information such as this please inform me of the procedures for collecting said reward.
I and my staff will provide methodology and any additional information about the suspected individual that we possess if that is your wish.
               Sincerely,
               Bradley Kinkaid

Sam read it over and said, "I think you covered all the bases.

Irvin said, "I suggest you provide your cell phone number."

I revised the letter to reflect that suggestion and we all agreed that it should get HS attention.

Sam and I went to the post office where I sent the letter priority/registered mail, and requested a delivery receipt.

That out of the way, we moved on to the phone numbers.

With some of the numbers it was a fairly simple matter to look them up in directories. We had all the calls Carolyn had placed or received for the seven day period prior to her disappearance. The number was 38, which seemed like a lot of phone conversations for such a short time period.

The ones we could find in directories Sam and I commenced to work on while Irvin continued to try to tie the other numbers to names.

Carolyn's parent's number reflected that they had talked four times during that week. We eliminated that one.

Pamela Whitehead's number appeared three times and we also eliminated that one.

It was after 2:00 pm and I wanted to be sure to catch Ellen Norton before she left the store, so I told Sam and Irvin, "I'm going to head on over to the convenience store to catch Ellen before she leaves for the day. I need time to convince her that we need to talk."

Sam asked, "You want me to come along."

"That might not be a bad idea. If I have to concoct some story about the bad guys you might come in handy."

"I'm not sure if that's a compliment or a putdown," Sam said laughing.

We made the trip to the store and arrived in time to catch her, even with the heavy customer load at that time of day.

Sam and I each grabbed a soda and when I paid for them I mentioned that I would like to have a word with her about a friend of a friend. I mentioned Pamela Whitehead, Bill Clampett, and Charles Inman, names I had gotten from the year book.

"It will have to wait until I get off, which is at 4:00," she said.

"No problem. We will wait," I said.

Chapter 10

When Ellen got off she met us outside.

"What do you want to talk about?" She asked.

She apparently was under the impression that what we wanted to talk about was one of her old classmates.

"Do you think we could go someplace a bit more private?" I asked.

"You've got to be kidding. I have no intention of going off with someone I don't know."

"Well, it's somewhat private and we really do need to talk." I took out my PI badge and in the process exposed the pistol in the shoulder holster."

"Can you give me some idea what this is about?" she asked.

"We are working for the store owner. He is missing a significant amount of money on a regular basis and hired us to see if we could find out how it is being done and who is doing it. We have been investigating all the store employees," I said.

"Trevor Whitmore is probably the one you want. He has been hitting on me and brags about how he can show me a good time. He certainly couldn't do that on what he makes at his job," she said.

"If you don't want to go someplace private, might I suggest a coffeehouse so we can discuss the matter more fully?" I asked.

"Okay, there's a place about three blocks down on the left side. It's called Bill's Restaurant. I will meet you there."

We climbed in our respective cars and headed to Bill's.

Once seated and with coffee in front of us I said. "We had already concluded that Trevor Whitmore was probably the thief. We now have to figure out how he is doing it because the books and inventories all tally. Any ideas about how he is managing to do that?"

"If he is fencing stolen goods, things like cigarettes come to mind, he could void a sale and replace however many packs he sold, pocketing the money. The register and inventory would still tally. We don't handle enough high dollar items to make that likely, but it is a way that it could be done. There's no way he could manipulate the gas pumps. Sodas and coffee aren't controlled all that well and that might be another avenue. I just don't know how he would be doing it, but he seems to have more money than a person in his position would have. He bought a new car recently, well, not a new car but newer and in much better shape than what he drove to that point."

"I thank you for that information. While we are on the subject, how can you afford the house you live in? It appears to be well above your station in life as well."

"I inherited it from an aunt. She died four years ago and didn't have any children. I had always been sort of her favorite and she left it to me. I also helped take care of her toward the end. She had cancer and it was really rough in the last few weeks."

"While what I told you was factual, I really wanted to talk to you about Carolyn Clayton."

"What about her?" she asked.

I could detect a bit of nervousness when I mentioned the name.

"You know that she disappeared five years ago?" I asked.

"Yes, I heard about that," she said.

"Her parents hired me to look into the matter since the police had not come up with any clues. I and my associates," I said, pointing to Sam, "managed to get a few leads that have established some facts that the police did not uncover."

"Like what?" she asked, now a bit more interested, at least it seemed that way to me.

"She had dinner with Pamela Whitehead on Saturday night before she was reported missing on Monday. Pamela said she was a bit distracted, I think distraught was the way she worded it. Something was bothering her, though she didn't confide in Pamela what it was. What's your connection to Carolyn?"

"How did you connect me to her?" she asked.

"Through the spirit of Carolyn," I said truthfully.

"You're kidding, right?"

"Not in the least. We work with a psychic and Carolyn's spirit appeared to her and gave the password to her e-mail files and your name. Since we knew who you were we first thought that she might be trying to help us solve the case of the missing money so that we could devote more time to looking into her disappearance. You worked for the store and it was a logical conclusion. The psychic said that she didn't think that was the case because no spirit who had contacted her previously provided information not related to the subject they wanted her to know about."

"You mean she can actually contact spirits?"

"No, it doesn't work that way. Spirits can contact her but the reverse is not true. She is in her sixties and has a doctoral degree in applied psychology. The story goes all the way back to her childhood and she has been contacted by numerous spirits over the years, always those seeking to help others in some manner. This is the second case I have worked on where spirits have provided information that helped move the case forward. In the previous case the lady in question had been murdered but her death was attributed to natural causes. The spirit insisted that she had been murdered and when we had the body exhumed she proved to be correct. She had been poisoned."

"I read about that in the paper. She actually came back from the dead and told the psychic that?"

"No, they don't come back from the dead. The spirit just makes a brief appearance and passes the message, then fades back to wherever they come from. I know it sounds kind of creepy, but I have had a spirit appear to me so I know it is possible."

"So that leads you to believe that I am somehow tied to Carolyn's disappearance?" Ellen asked.

"That's about the size of it. We desperately need to know if you had any contact with her after high school. She is obviously dead or her spirit couldn't have made an appearance. Her parents are anxious to find out for sure. That's why they hired me."

Ellen took a deep breath, preparing herself to reveal what part she played in Carolyn's last days. "I don't know if you are aware, but I was arrested a couple of years out of high school. I

Case Files of Bradley Kinkaid

ran with a pretty rough bunch sometimes and got into drugs. We had parties at which marijuana and some other stuff was available. I tried marijuana and meth. The meth almost got me hooked but I was arrested for possession. The judge took pity on me and got me into a halfway house where I could see and appreciate where my path was leading."

"I got through that and haven't touched any kind of drugs since. I even chew up aspirin to make sure it is what the package says," she finished with a chuckle.

"We know about the arrest and that it was dismissed. But that still doesn't explain your connection to Carolyn Clayton," I said.

"In Carolyn's final year of college she got into the drug culture. She tried a couple of the lesser evils and found them to be very addictive. She knew about my arrest and one day she called me right out of the blue. You have to understand that she and I didn't run with the same crowd in high school, and that had been four years earlier anyway. She said that she was going to Europe for her graduation trip but that she would like to talk with me when she got back. I agreed."

"She called, I think it was late July, and asked if we could meet. I invited her to the house here and we talked a long time that evening and night. She told me about how she had done pretty much as I had and wanted to know the best way to get rid of the habit once and for all. The recovering addict program, though neither of us were what you call addicts, is very similar to the AA program. You know, the 'once an alcoholic, always an alcoholic'.

"The one positive thing with both of us is that we had not used often enough to get really hooked. I relayed some of the things I had learned at the halfway house that I think helped both of us. It's kind of hard to explain to someone who has never been hooked on something."

"We still didn't travel in the same social circles, but we vowed to meet at least monthly to reaffirm to each other that we were still clean. Sometimes we met at her place, sometimes at

80

mine. Other times we had dinner out. She really was a sweet and caring person," Ellen said.

"So what has this to do with her disappearance?" I asked.

"Just hold your horses, I will get to that," she said.

"We had been meeting for about a year and were at her place that time. She was doing a microwave lasagna and we were talking about guys, which girls often do. She told me about and brief affair she had while on her graduation trip. She said the guy was a bit older but wasn't anything like she thought he would be. He was rough with her, though not sadistic, more, she said, like he was used to getting his way without question."

"They were together on his yacht the two nights before she was to leave. They had had several drinks and the sex did not take long. Omar, he called himself fell asleep right away. Carolyn said she went into the bathroom and closed the door. Omar had emptied his pockets and put everything on the shelf. She looked in his wallet and found that Omar was not his name. His name was Abdul Fahad Sarraf."

"She was enamored with the yacht and his easy manner with money. She wanted a picture of him but didn't think it would be a good idea to ask him about that particular subject. The next night, which would have been the night before she left, she saw him enter one of the restaurants they had dined at and followed to the door a few minutes later. As she entered she saw him sitting at a table with another man and quickly snapped a picture with her phone. She showed me the picture and I got the shock of my life. I had been following the suicide bombings in London and one of the bombers was staring right at me from the picture."

"That's one of the suicide bombers in the London attacks" I gasped.

Carolyn could hardly believe it. We went to her computer and read an article about the bombings which had pictures of all four. "By golly, it is him," she said. "What would Sarraf be doing having dinner with someone like that unless..." she couldn't finish the sentence.

"You don't believe this could have been a chance meeting, do you, I asked?"

"I don't think so. 'Omar' wasn't the type to just join someone without prior arrangements," Carolyn said.

"What are you going to do? I'm sure the authorities would like to have that picture."

"What if I turned it over to the government and he was completely innocent? I would hate to implicate an innocent man in something like that," Carolyn said.

"We met at my place in August. I asked Carolyn what she decided to do about the picture. Nothing for the moment, she answered."

"In September we had dinner at a restaurant. The subject of the picture didn't come up. Then when we met at her house again in October she told me she was frightened. She thought she was being followed. I suspect that she had somehow made contact with Sarraf and that might be the explanation and told her as much."

"What can he do, she asked? It now appears that you and I both know what he could and probably did do," Ellen finished the narrative.

"So you think she contacted Sarraf and he had her killed?"

"I don't see any other explanation. I have had this bottled up inside me for five years. I think about it over and over and cannot come up with any other explanation for her disappearance. I thought about going to the police with what I know, but figured that would put me in the line of fire. I know that's a coward's way out, but I am not a very brave person. Knowing I had the possession charge on the record also influenced my inaction," Ellen said.

"How much time elapsed between your last meeting with Ellen and her disappearance?" I asked.

"We met the last week of October, so the time in November she disappeared and that date would be it."

"Did she manage to stay off the drugs?"

"Yes, I believe she did. One addict can usually tell when another addict is lying about it. It's in the eyes and mannerisms. I think she was clean right up until the end."

"We had figured a lot of this out. We passed the picture and identity of Sarraf to Homeland Security. While I am happy to help with the national security aspect, I really wanted to find something that would put us on the scent of the killers or abductors," I said.

"Carolyn was a pretty thorough person. She worked in the financial industry and those folks are fanatics about the little things. If she was being followed and could get a license number then she would do that. I don't know what she would do once she had it, but I am sure that if she could identify a car she would have filed the number some place," Ellen said.

"I guess that means we are going to have to open the rest of the crates containing her household furnishings," Sam said.

"I appreciate your being so open with us. Now if we can only catch Trevor in the act," I said.

"The ceiling in the store looks like a drop ceiling, which it is, but not many people know that the area above is covered with plywood. You might think about having someone climb up there and spend the night watching him," Ellen suggested.

"That's a thought. I might bring that up with the owner," I said. "Might I have your cell phone number? We have a list of all the calls Carolyn made in what was apparently the final week of her life. If I have yours it will help to eliminate known parties."

"Will you call me anyway and let me know what you learn?"

"Yes, I will do that."

On that note we went our separate ways.

Chapter 11

On the drive back home I told Sam, "I am going to have to brief the Claytons. I want to keep the affair out of it but I don't know if that is the right thing to do. They paid for the efforts that uncovered the facts and I don't feel right keeping it secret from them."

"I know where you are coming from. If they have this vision of their daughter as the unrequited virgin it will certainly burst their bubble," Sam replied.

"I don't believe they are that prudish. I think I am going to have to lay it all out for them, including the drugs and Ellen's involvement."

"Maybe I should skip that meeting," Sam said.

"It might be better if I give that brief solo. I don't believe they would react negatively, but I have been wrong before. You could be uncrating her apartment belongings while I do the brief," I said.

"Tha's rat. Make the nigger do the dirty work," Sam said.

"I will be happy to do the unpacking while you do the brief," I said.

"Tha's awright. I do da nigga work boss," Sam said with a hardy laugh.

"All that training at UCLA and you still play the buffoon," I said.

"Just so you know that I am playing the part," Sam said.

"We need to bring Lillian up to date, and we also have to think about letting the police know what we have found out." I was thinking out loud and Sam knew I didn't expect a response.

When we were back at the house I replayed the conversation with Ellen Norton. "She didn't say it in so many words, but I got the impression that she thinks Carolyn got in touch with Omar, aka Abdul Fahad Sarraf and told him about the picture. She said Carolyn told her that she was being followed in the weeks leading up to her disappearance."

"That may be true, but wouldn't you think that someone like Sarraf would at least have enough sense to instruct someone detailed to kill her over the picture to make sure all copies were destroyed?" Irvin asked.

"Yes, I would think so. It is possible that Carolyn told Sarraf that what she sent him was the only copy, but he would have to be mentally challenged to take that as gospel. The busy apartment complex could have played a role in the people assigned to take care of the matter not being too thorough. I know that the lady directly across from her keeps her blinds open until they go to bed, sometimes after 11:00 pm. I just don't know the reason."

"It could be because they needed a password to get on the computer, and you know how long it took me to do that," Irvin replied.

"Why not just disconnect the computer and take the tower?" I asked.

"Maybe limited time? Could be that something spooked them while they were in the apartment. The only factual part of the story is that they didn't take it and now it is going to come back to bite old Abdul on the back side," Sam offered.

My cell phone rang and I looked at the caller ID. It was blocked so I answered. "Brad Kinkaid," I said.

"Mr. Kinkaid, this is the Director of Homeland Security. I received your very unusual letter and wonder if you might be willing to come to Washington to discuss it?" she asked.

Before I had a chance to reply she continued, "The government will provide transportation of course."

"When and where?" I replied.

"If you could be at the LA airport at 9:00 am tomorrow I will have transportation arranged. Just go to the security checkpoint and identify yourself. The agents on duty will know what to do," she said.

"I will have another person with me," I said.

"What's his name?"

"Sam Rathbone," I said.

"I look forward to seeing you tomorrow," she said and hung up.

"Well Sam, looks like you and I are going to meet the Director of Homeland Security."

"How are we going to get there?"

"I have no idea. She said to be at the security checkpoint at LAX at 9:00 am and they would know what to do. I hope it isn't to kidnap us," I said jokingly.

"Are you going to take your pistol?"

"Why not. If HS is arranging the flight they can certainly make provisions for our weapons."

"I believe Lillian is next on our agenda. Looks like take-out again tonight."

I called and told her we were coming over with food if that met her approval. She was delighted and said to get chicken again. She never seemed to tire of fried chicken.

When we got there and settled in I told her that her instincts had been right about Ellen Norton, and what she had told us.

"Well my instincts were not as good as you imagine because Merle and I discussed the matter and thought that she might be part of the plan to abduct/kill Carolyn," she said.

"The read I got was that she was being entirely truthful."

I replayed the entire conversation with Ellen with Sam's help.

When I finished Lillian said, "That makes more sense than what Merle and I came up with. It also explains what Pamela said about Carolyn being distraught on that Saturday night."

"On another note, Sam and I are going to Washington tomorrow to meet with the HS Director. She called this afternoon and said she would arrange transportation if we would come to discuss the tie in of Sarraf to terrorism."

"I sent them a letter with skimpy details to find out if there was a reward offered for that kind of information and the phone call was the result. I want your opinion on something else as well. I am going to have to brief the Clayton's and with all that we have found out I think I have to let them know about the affair Carolyn had with Abdul. Do you agree?"

86

Lillian thought it over for a few seconds. "I think it is only fair that you tell them everything you found and how. It might come as a shock to them, but parents do know that their offspring have sexual drives and it would not devastate them. I believe you need to cover everything, even the drug thing and the association with Ellen. Parents are not as ignorant about their kid's affairs as some people think. It's all water under the bridge, and while it might taint their memory of her it is relevant to the case."

"I feel the same, so when I get back I will give them a thorough briefing," I said.

"So Ellen also confirmed your suspicion about Trevor on the other case."

"Yes. She thinks he lives beyond his means and sees no other source for additional income. I think he's our guy. We now need to figure out how he is skimming the money."

When we left Lillian's I felt better about the situation.

We hit the sack early so as to fight the traffic into the airport the next morning. We were up at 5:30 am and on the road by six. If you have not driven in LA during rush hour you might not understand why we would leave three hours before an appointment when the location was only an hour away. It was one of the things I didn't like about the city.

We made it on time and I parked in the short term lot rather than the more distant long-term area. I figured we would be back by tomorrow and a few bucks wouldn't make a lot of difference.

When we got to the security checkpoint I informed the agent who we were and he asked for ID. "You should also know that we are armed," I said.

"You're going to be on a government plane so the normal restrictions will not apply, unless your escort feels threatened," he said with a laugh. "With the Director of HS personally laying this on I don't think he will feel threatened."

We were handed off to another agent who escorted us around the metal detectors and down the corridor to a side door which said official business only. The agent had to use a key card to open the door. He led us to an SUV with TSA stenciled on the side and back and motioned us into the vehicle. He told the driver that was his package and to deliver us to the Gulfstream.

We were taken to a sleek business jet with USAF markings and shown aboard. A gentleman in civilian clothing met us at the doorway and introduced himself as Ansel Devlin. "I'm the Director's right hand man. We have known each other a long time and she sends me on chores she wants to keep on the quiet side. I see a bulge in the jacket. Are both of you armed?"

"Yes," I said, answering for both of us.

"Being from Arizona I am not surprised. I remember you from your playing days at ASU," he said to me. He then turned to Sam and said, "And with your size I would guess that you have a bit of experience on the gridiron as well."

Sam laughed. It was clear that he really liked Ansel. "I played for UCLA, then signed a pro contract. I got hurt bad enough to end my playing days before even playing a down in a regular game. I had a good insurance settlement, so all was not in vain."

"Smart man. Insurance is a great thing when you really need it. Course, none of us like paying the premiums until the need does arise. You guys are kind of like insurance. What the Director wants to do is make sure her insurance is top notch before she pays the premium for something that she may never need, but might just possibly find a need in the future."

"Well that certainly explains that," Sam said.

Ansel laughed so hard he almost cried. "I can't get into what she wants to talk about, not that I would know anyway. Just relax and enjoy the flight. There's booze if you want it and the galley has some prepared stuff, but it's not gourmet. We should be arriving around 2:30 and a car will take us directly to Nebraska Avenue, where the headquarters is located. We have made arrangements to put you up at a good hotel just up the road in Bethesda."

"Wind up the rubber bands," he said to the flight attendant, who relayed the word to the cockpit.

We settled into spacious seats and relaxed and made small talk with Ansel until we landed at Washington National Airport.

The ride to Nebraska Avenue took longer than normal because of the traffic that was beginning to build, though still nothing like LA.

It was close to 4:00 pm when we arrived. As we entered the building there was a metal detector that most people have to go through, but Ansel waved us around it and said, "They're with me," as if the fact meant that we could walk around armed like the rest of the staff.

He took us directly to the office of the Director. Since it was near the close of normal business hours she didn't have anyone in the office, so we went right in.

Ansel made the introductions and the Director said to him, "See if you can locate Weatherly and Lomax."

While Ansel was gone she said, "Tell me about the letter you sent."

"Well, the letter lays out the facts. We discovered that Sarraf had contact with one of the London bombers about a year before the incident, in Cannes. We then got the identity of the other man and that's in the letter as well. I thought that if a direct tie between the two was enough evidence to establish that Sarraf was a possible terrorist suspect, then there might be a reward offered," I said.

Ansel came back in with the two the Director had asked him to locate. He had not been gone long enough to have strayed very far from the office so he must have had them standing by.

Introductions were made and we moved to a small conference table in the Director's office.

"We were just talking about the letter Mr. Kinkaid sent and why. Would you mind going over it again Mr. Kinkaid?"

"Call me Bradley or Brad," I said, and reiterated what I had told the Director.

"How did you identify Mr. Sarraf?" Lomax asked.

"We are working on a missing person case in Los Angeles, and the young lady in question knew Sarraf. She had met him in

Cannes while on a graduation trip to Europe. She is the one who took the picture. From her files we knew that he owned a yacht, so I asked the local police department, which is Westlake, to ask the authorities in Cannes if they could provide a list of all the yachts in Cannes during the time in question. They did and we eliminated all the non-Arabic owners and only had a handful to look into. We did a computer search of maritime web sites and tied the registration numbers to names. We then did another search of the names and got information on each of the individuals in question. The same man in the picture showed up under the name Abdul Fahad Sarraf."

"You didn't know his name before?" Weatherly asked.

"No. Our missing person knew him as Omar Sharique. We didn't even waste time trying to run that name down," I said.

"Why not," the Director asked.

"Mostly because of the circumstances under which our missing person met him. The real reason was because he told our missing person that he was going to Portsmouth, England when he left Cannes. If he was involved in the London attacks as I suspect he would not use his real name with a person unknown to him until that time."

"I guess that makes sense in a way," Weatherly said.

"What is your interest in him?" the Director asked.

"I believe he had the young lady we are searching for killed," I said.

"Is that just a guess, or do you have something solid that leads you to believe such is the case?" she asked.

"It's kind of a long story but we have a witness who was aware that the man in the picture with the bomber was Sarraf, though she didn't know his name. Carolyn Clayton, the missing person, was showing her pictures of her European trip shortly after the bombings and she recognized the bomber, which Carolyn had not connected at the time. She advised Carolyn to go to the authorities but Carolyn, who was emotionally involved with Sarraf insisted that it could be coincidence and that it would be morally wrong to place an innocent person under suspicion. They dropped the subject. When they next met, which was a month later, Carolyn told her friend that she thought she was being followed. A close friend, who had dinner with Carolyn on the Saturday night before she disappeared, told us that Carolyn seem distraught. She mentioned the fact to Carolyn and she perked up, but said that it was a personal matter. That was the last contact anyone had with Carolyn to our knowledge," I finished.

"Where did you come up with the information that resulted in what you just told us?" Lomax asked.

"Just plain old detective work. I got the file from the Westlake police department, which was nothing more than an address and statements from the parents of the missing girl, and a statement from the apartment manager. We went back over all they had done and knocked on some doors. We found out enough to get a feel for the kind of person she was. The police had no reason to believe that Carolyn disappeared from her apartment but dusted for prints anyway. They didn't find anything out of the ordinary and later the parents, who live near Malibu, had her belongings packed up and moved to their house. Five years later the boxes are still stored in their garage. An interview with an elderly lady who visited with Carolyn occasionally mentioned her computer in the corner of the living room."

"I have on my staff a young man who is very good with computers and he suggested that the computer might yield some useful information if he could get into the files. I discussed the matter with the parents and they allowed us to take the computer. Once my man managed to get into the password protected computer we went through her address book and called the people listed, at least the ones we could reach. One of the people was a childhood friend who still lived in the area. We met with her and got the description of Carolyn's mood on that Saturday night before she disappeared."

"This is the point at which I have to ask you if you believe in ghosts," I said and paused.

They all looked at me waiting for me to continue.

"Well, do you?"

The Director said, "I have never had any reason to, but on the other hand, I have never had any reason not to. Is there a specific reason for that question?"

"Yes," I answered and turned to the others. "How about you gentlemen? Do you believe in ghosts?"

Two shook their heads no, but Ansel kind of shrugged. He obviously wanted to say yes but didn't want to be the odd man out.

"I work with a psychic. I am not talking about the kind you see in the movies, or on the billboards. This is a true psychic. I recently worked on another case where the victim of foul play appeared to her and told her that she was murdered, even though the autopsy said death by natural causes. The information she provided helped us solve a smuggling case that had been in operation for years."

"I read about that. I don't remember seeing anything about a psychic though," Lomax said.

"Would you want something like that in the paper?" I asked, "Unless you were a scam artist and were looking for marks."

"I don't suppose I would," he agreed.

"Anyway. We were stumped trying to get into the e-mail files on Carolyn's computer. We felt that the e-mail account was the key to identifying Omar."

"Lillian, the psychic, had a vision in which Carolyn appeared and said 'ambrosia 13' then she said, 'Ellen Norton'. Lillian called me and passed the information on. My computer guy tried ambrosia 13 for the password, and it worked."

"The name didn't have any meaning to Lillian, but it did to me. We are working on another case, trying to figure out how a convenience store is being bilked without the cameras or books picking it up. Ellen Norton is an employee and was one of our suspects. In running the name down we found that she had gone to the same high school as Carolyn. I thought at first the spirit was telling me that Ellen Norton was the guilty party in the theft. When we learned that she had been a high school classmate of our missing person we started looking in that direction. Lillian, who has experienced ghostly appearances since she was a child, said that spirits do not usually stray from the very narrow confines of their own misfortunes. She thought that there was a connection between Carolyn and Ellen that we did not know about."

"That turned out to be the case, and while I will not bore you with all the details, led to the recognition of the bomber in the picture you have."

"Other than seeking a reward for the information, what are you hoping to get out of this?" the Director asked.

"I believe Sarraf was behind the murder of our client's daughter, and I would love to be able to tie him to the people who did the dirty work. I also would like to put the perpetrators behind bars," I said.

"As to the reward, the British still have a £100,000 reward offer for information leading to the person behind the attacks in 2005. I don't know if this will satisfy their requirements, but I believe it will. You are assuming that your missing person called Sarraf and said something like, 'Gee, do you know the guy you were having dinner with in Cannes was one of the London bombers'."

"That's one theory, though I don't know how she would have identified him to place the call. I think he then had her followed to try to determine if anyone else knew what she told him, and eventually had her killed," I said.

"Do you plan to stay on this guy's trail?" she asked.

"What else can I do? I feel he is the prime suspect, perhaps the only one at this point," I said.

"Do you plan to go to Saudi Arabia to pursue your theory?"

"I don't think my client would spring for that kind of money," I said.

"What if someone else paid for the trip, and even paid for your time while you were looking into the matter?" she asked.

"What do you have in mind?"

"Mr. Weatherly is with the Central Intelligence Agency. They have the charter for intelligence collection outside our borders. He thinks that with your background, and yes we checked you out, that you will be more likely to find something to tie Sarraf to terrorism than his own people."

"First, I am impressed that you got as far as you have with this case, since the police had the first shot and didn't have any clues. Second, I know more about the last case you worked on than I let on. I know that without you the smuggling ring would still be in operation. So, if you agree to our proposal you can take as many of your people as you feel you need and try to get the goods on Sarraf on his own turf. We, the CIA, will pay your normal fees, plus provide living expenses and travel. We will also provide whatever weapons you need and prepaid credit cards for any purchases you need to make. I don't want to let too many people know about this, but if you get in a jam I will have procedures in place to bail you out. If you are agreeable we can get together to work out the details at a later time."

I turned to Sam, "It appears that your good reason is at hand."

"What does that mean?" Weatherly asked.

"We were discussing the possibility of going to Saudi Arabia and my friend said that he would not go without some very compelling reason," I said.

Weatherly laughed. "Can't say that I blame him."

"You do know that all my associates are black?" I asked.

"That will be a positive rather than a negative. The Saudi's use a lot of Somali's and other people of color to work their oil fields and such."

"I will need to discuss the matter with the others before I give you a decision," I said.

Weatherly handed me a business card and said, "Call me when you make a decision and we will take it from there."

The meeting broke up and Lomax and Weatherly went their own ways.

After they left the Director said to me, "I really believe the British will cough up the money. I know that the evidence is somewhat circumstantial, but it is more of a lead than they have after five years of looking and it gives them a definite direction in which to look. I will personally talk with the people concerned and let you know what comes of it. Ansel will take you to your hotel and arrange transportation for you tomorrow. It's nice to see a fellow Arizonan in the thick of the battle."

We spent the night in a Marriott and flew back to LA the following day.

Chapter 12

With the time difference we arrived back in LA before noon. I called Lillian first and asked if Sam and I could come by later in the afternoon. We set a time and I asked Irvin if he knew where James was.

"He might be talking to the store owner. They have enough documentation to show that Trevor is probably the thief. I believe he wants to watch the place from the ceiling location Ellen told you guys about," he replied.

I called James' cell number and he answered on the first ring.

"What are you doing now?"

"Just left a meeting with the store owner. I am going to have Matt spend the night in the attic. I'm about to set that up now."

"Once you get it ironed out met me back at the house. I have to go to see Lillian and then the Claytons, so there's no rush," I said.

"You want to go with us to see Lillian?" I asked Irvin.

"Not much point in my being there if we are going to have our own meeting later this evening," he said.

Sam and I headed for Burbank.

Once there I went over the meeting with DHS and told them what the CIA had offered. "It gives us a chance to try to nail Sarraf for the killing of Carolyn but I think that is a real long shot. If he is a terrorist supporter as we suspect and we can pin that on him it will be just as good. The British in particular won't go to the Saudi's and ask that he be extradited. They will go for the ultimate solution."

"If you decide to do it I suggest you charge them considerably more than you would for work here in the states. Then there's the extra hazards associated with the case," Lillian said. "Who are you going to take with you?"

"James, Sam, and Irvin. We still haven't wrapped up the case for the convenience store owner yet and Matt and Larry will have to do that. If we decide to go to Saudi Arabia I am going to have them stay at the house, just so someone's there," I said.

I called the Clayton's and told them we would be there after dinner if that fit their schedule. Mrs. Clayton invited us for dinner but we figured it would be best to grab a bite on the way over.

We got there just after 7:00 and took Roberta up on the offer of coffee and dessert. The table had been cleared and we sat around it.

"Some of what I am going to tell you I debated with myself if it was relevant. In the end I decided that you needed to know everything we have found out, even though some of it you will find distasteful."

I recounted all that we had done and how we came upon the information that led to each disclosure. It took the better part of an hour. I even told them about the meeting with DHS and the offer from the CIA. "I don't believe I was supposed to mention the last, but I want you to know that we didn't just blow you off and went on to other things."

"Ellen Norton feels that Carolyn would have written down any license numbers associated with the people she thought were following her. From what we have been able to piece together I tend to agree with her assessment. In that regard I want to have Matt and Larry carefully go through all of the things from her apartment. It is just possible that they will find something tucked into a different purse, or even in one of the drawers. If you have no objections, since everything is here, I want them to do it here," I said.

Mrs. Clayton said, "We knew that she was sexually active from birth control pills I saw in her medicine cabinet. The drugs is a shock, but I am glad she sought help. I still want to see whoever is responsible for what you seem to have accepted as her death, caught and punished, so as far as I am concerned you are still on the case."

"I agree whole heartedly," Harry said.

"I don't know how long we will be out of touch, but I will contact you at the earliest opportunity, especially if we make any progress," I said.

Sam and I went back to the house and got together with James and Irvin. I outlined the proposal of the CIA and asked them what they thought about it.

"How do you propose to use us? You do realize that it's going to be difficult for us to blend in," James said.

"No problem," Sam said. "We're going to be Somali's working in the oil fields, or wherever we can find jobs that look like ways to learn something worthwhile."

James looked at Irvin, who shrugged his shoulders. "Will we have weapons?"

"The CIA will provide whatever we tell them we need, up to and including C-4 or shoulder fired missiles," I told them. "It really is no more dangerous than living in LA if you conform to their social standards. You will have to pray four times a day and probably wear robes, except if you happen to be working in the oil fields, then you will probably wear clothing provided by your employer," I said.

"Will we get an increase in pay?" James asked.

I laughed. "I am going to charge them about twice what we would charge here, and if they don't balk I will also ask for hazardous duty pay. They will be paying for everything and it will probably come out of their black budget, which means they don't have to account for it to the government controllers. And not to be forgotten, DHS thinks she can convince the British to pay us for the information we provided. The reward is £100,000, which is about half again as much in dollars. That, if it happens will be split among us as bonus money, after taxes, of course."

"Then I guess we are in," James said.

"Make sure Matt and Larry have a handle on the convenience store job and tell the owner that Larry will be the point of contact," I said to James.

"I will call Weatherly back tomorrow afternoon and tell him our decision. There's a ton of stuff that will be required but we will let the CIA worry about that," I finished.

I slept better that night than I had in a long time.

The next morning James got a call from Matt.

He had observed Trevor all night and not only had the goods on him but an accomplice as well.

The accomplice was bringing cigarettes by the carton into the store and Trevor stored them under the counter. When someone bought cigarettes he didn't ring them up if the customer was paying cash, which was the case about 75 percent of the time. If he rang them up he simply voided the sale after the customer left. He then replaced the number of packages of cigarettes he had sold onto the shelves.

Matt kept count during his shift and counted 93 cigarette sales, some for multiple packs. That came to over $500 in a single night, probably more due to multiple item sales.

Matt told James, "After the accomplice delivered the cigarettes they reset the security cameras to erase his presence. It's a pretty slick operation. The cigarettes probably come from a robbery someplace else and since they have the California tax stamps it is easy to get rid of them."

"Did you get it on film?" James asked.

"Yes, on my phone camera. The quality is not all that great. I had to hold the lens over the hole in the drop ceiling I had made to observe through. It is good enough to see what was happening and both individuals are identifiable."

"Get in touch with the client and show him what you have. If he wants to catch them in the act you guys can set something up with the police to do what you did in the attic. I think our part in this is over. Come on back to the house after you talk to the owner. We have some other things to discuss," James told him.

Irvin and I followed the conversation from James' side and pretty much knew what they had said.

"I'm glad we were able to wrap that up before we leave. I don't want Matt and Larry committing the company to anything major in our absence, so we will need to leave specific guidelines for them on the kinds of things they can do on their own," I said.

"I also want them to know that they can call Lillian for guidance and help if they should need either."

I placed the call to Weatherly and told him that four of us would go to Saudi Arabia. "I have a few loose ends to tie up, but we should be in Washington day after tomorrow."

"Call me when you get in. Don't get hotel rooms. I will handle arrangements for all of you," he said.

Later in the afternoon I received another call from DHS.

"The Brits seemed to think the information you provided was good enough to qualify for the reward, but they want to talk to you in person."

"We will be coming to Washington on the other matter day after tomorrow. Can they do the meet in Washington?"

"I will check into that and get back to you."

"Looks like we will be getting the reward money from the British. They want to talk, so I will try to set that up while we are in Washington. Irvin, be sure to bring your laptop," I said.

"It's like my American Express card, I never go anyplace without it," he replied.

"If there's anything you need to do here, get it taken care of tomorrow. Plan on being gone for at least a month. I think the schedule will be at our discretion. If we need more time they will go along. If we find what we are looking for in less time the trip will be shorter."

The next day was busy for all of us, taking care of personal matters.

DHS called back and said someone from the British Embassy would be in touch through Weatherly after our arrival.

I called Lillian and brought her up to date and told her that the government would probably issue us satellite phones, and that if they did I would call and give her the number.

Weatherly had arranged tickets for us on U.S. Airways and all we had to do was check in. Since the government was going to provide weapons for us we elected to leave ours at home.

The flight to Washington was not nearly as enjoyable as the previous one, especially for Sam.

It was after 6:00 when we arrived and I figured it would be hard to get Weatherly on the line, but he had made the flight arrangements and knew when we were to land. He met us personally and, along with another car, took us to what the spooks call a safe house. It was located in the country not too far from where we landed at Dulles airport.

The house was a two story horse farm, complete with animals and a four foot high rock fence that must have been built a couple of centuries in the past. It was a very picturesque place and had six bedrooms, four on the second floor, and two on the ground floor. It had a wraparound covered porch and would bring a lot of money on the real estate market.

There was a cook and a caretaker, or handyman, both armed.

Bud and Nell were the only names given and we responded with our first names, though they probably knew who we were and it didn't make a lot of difference to me anyway.

We were assigned bedrooms and Weatherly said that after we had time to freshen up a bit we would talk.

The cook had prepared a plate of sandwiches and had placed a pitcher of lemonade and another of tea on the table.

When we arrived at the table she said, "There's beer or stronger stuff if you would prefer."

Sam and James attacked the sandwiches with gusto. Irvin and I only ate one each. Sam didn't stop until the platter was empty.

"Does he eat like that all the time?" the cook asked.

"Pretty much. He has a lot of cells to feed," I replied.

Once the table was cleaned the cook went back into the kitchen and Weatherly started his briefing. "I am the director of operations for the Middle East. I have made a list of all the things you will need. Look it over and tell me what to add or change. I have the forms for passports. We will need to decide if you are going to use your real names or some aliases. You guys decide that among yourselves. Let me know what type weapons you prefer and how much ammunition you will need. You can purchase local clothing after you arrive. Not that I doubt your qualifications, but while the paperwork is being taken care of I want to send you to our training facility to get some familiarization with our methods. Each of you will receive a satellite phone. Those will be provided to you when you get where you are going. Keep your regular cell phones for now."

"Brad, the Brits want to have a word with you. I will bring a couple of them out here in the morning. If you can decide on the names you want on the passports I can get that process started tomorrow."

"If we are masquerading as Somali's or Ethiopians, wouldn't it make sense to have passports from those countries, and if the Saudi's require them, work permits?" Sam asked.

"Of course that is true, but you will enter the country under your American passports, but under aliases if you so desire. You will be provided the documents you suggested once you are in Saudi Arabia, along with weapons and any other support equipment you need."

"None of what we are doing will be documented anywhere in our files. The money for the operation comes from discretionary funds that do not require any accounting or justification of expenditures. You will each be paid $1,000 per day, and if this goes as we hope, considerable bonuses."

"What about the language problem?" Irvin asked.

"We can give you a cram course, maybe two days, to familiarize you with the words and phrases that are of interest. Brad probably already has that from his time in Iraq. There simply isn't time to go through an intensive language program. You guys will probably be working with those you are impersonating and should be able to pick up some of the language. I don't know how you will get around the problem once you are on the ground over there."

"Sam's big enough to speak whatever language he wants, but James and I can't use that same tactic," Irvin said.

James said, "I spent a year over there, so I know some phrases and can probably understand enough to get the gist of what someone is talking about. You could just play mute," he said to Irvin.

Irvin gave him the finger, though the thought had some merit.

We spent some time looking over the list Weatherly provided.

"What do you guys think about just using our real names to get there? That way there's less likelihood that we will be tripped up over some small thing we should know about an alias but don't," I said.

"We're not running from anyone, so I can't see that it would hurt anything," Sam replied.

"Other than personal weapons we are not going to have any clue as to what we need until we get there," I said.

"Then let's just worry about the passports for now. I will have each of you sign the form and have someone process them tomorrow. It will probably take two days, but you will be at the training facility anyway, so there's no rush. I will leave you for now, but I will return in the morning with the Brits, say 9:00 am."

After weatherly left we went outside and walked around the property. I saw a couple of horses and walked toward them automatically, having been raised on a ranch.

Sam asked, "What are you doing?"

"Just gonna say hello to the horses. I might even go for a short ride around the property," I answered.

"They don't even have saddles," Irvin observed.

"You don't need a saddle to ride. The Indians never used saddles and they were some of the most adept riders ever," I replied.

The horses were pretty tame and walked toward us as we walked toward them. I could see that the other three were nervous, so I patted the nearest on the head and rubbed her neck. She nickered and nudged me with her head.

"Sorry old girl, I don't have any treats. Maybe later."

I grabbed her mane and vaulted onto her back. She shied a bit but settled down quickly. I used my boots to nudge her forward and she complied. I hadn't ridden bareback in quite some time, but it's like riding a bicycle, once you learn the skill stays with you.

I kicked her a bit and she settled into an easy canter. I rode the perimeter of the property until I got back to the others, who were still standing there staring warily at the other horse.

I slid off the mare and asked if anyone wanted to give it a try.

The answer was a chorus of no's.

We went back into the house and I got a couple of carrots out of the refrigerator and went back out to the horses and gave each of them one.

We turned in early and had breakfast, a hearty one in consideration of Sam, before Weatherly arrived.

The Brits were introduced and we got right down to business.

"The Crown wants to thank you for the information you provided that just might help us to get to those behind the dastardly attacks in London in 2005," he said.

He opened his briefcase and took out a bank draft for £100,000 and handed it to me.

"That out of the way," he continued, "we would like to know everything you can tell us about Sarraf."

Weatherly had heard the story enough that he went into the kitchen in search of coffee as I started the narration.

It took almost an hour, and when I had finished there were questions that took another half hour. I neglected to mention the ghost in the story and they wondered how I had gotten a line on Ellen Norton.

I explained that they wouldn't believe the method so I had not mentioned it.

They were insistent, so I told them about Lillian and how she had a nighttime visit from the ghost of the lady who disappeared.

"Why did you think we would not believe it?" one of them asked.

"Well, most people simply think it is too ludicrous to be true if they have not had some exposure to the supernatural," I said.

"I must admit that I have had some experience in that field. I was raised in an old place that had ghosts. They didn't appear so we could see them, but strange thing were the norm rather than the exception. Pots and pans falling off their hooks, curtains moving when no breeze was present, and an odd shrieking at times."

I explained that Lillian had been raised in Pennsylvania where belief in the supernatural was very prevalent, and that she had been having the occasional contact with spirits for most of her life. I told them about the way we solved the smuggling case and confided that the victim in that murder had appeared to me as well.

"Apparently her info was right on the money old boy, and you can't argue with that," he said.

"Now what's the plan when you chaps get to turban land?"

"We really don't have one. I suppose the primary purpose is to try to tie Sarraf to other known or suspected terrorist backers. Since my friends are black we thought they might fit in as Somali's or Ethiopians. We could try to get Sam into the oil fields owned by Sarraf, and I thought Irvin and James might find some work close enough for us to keep an eye on what goes on around Sarraf's compound. We simply won't know until we get there. The language barrier is going to be a major problem."

"I have some satellite footage of his residence. You will be able to review that over the next couple of days," Weatherly said.

"Would it be asking too much to have a couple of my chaps on scene to assist if needed? They can be doing their own snooping while they are there, and I will make sure one or both of them speak the lingo," Nick asked.

"I don't have a problem with it. We still don't know how Brad is going to fit in," Weatherly said.

"He's good with horses," Sam said. "If they have horses he could become a stable hand or something like that."

"That will have to wait until you get there. The satellite footage might give you some ideas."

"I already had a look on Google Earth," Irvin said.

"What did it look like?" I asked.

"No horses unless they keep them in their courtyards. The compound is on the outskirts of the city."

"We will think of something," I said.

I waved the check around briefly. "I suppose I am going to have to pay taxes on this," I said.

"That's up to your government," Nick said.

"Why don't we route you through London on your way over and Nick can get together with you there and iron out the details," Weatherly said.

We were driven to a place near Williamsburg, Virginia and spent two days firing weapons and getting some language instruction.

Weatherly had someone pick us up and take us back to the same place we had stayed when we arrived.

He and two others met us there the following morning with the passports, pre-paid credit cards and several hundred dollars in cash. Weatherly told us the name of the man we would need to contact and gave us a phone number for him.

"Donald will give you everything you need. If you need something that he did not provide, ask for it. He will have weapons and satellite phones for each of you."

We caught an afternoon British Airways flight and were in London late that night. It was actually the next day, since it was after 1:00 am.

As we started to go through the customs line Nick showed up and walked us past the line of entering travelers and told us to give our baggage claims to the customs agent he had in tow. "He'll have them sent to the hotel where you will be staying," he said.

Nick drove us to a nice hotel. It wasn't a Hilton, but it wasn't a dump either. "I already signed you in and took care of the bill. I doubled you up with two beds per room and a connecting door," he said.

When we got to the rooms two other men were already there. "These gentlemen are Colin and John. Both speak Arabic, the kind spoken in Saudi Arabia, and will be there if you should need any assistance. I don't suppose you have been given authority to take him out if you feel it is warranted?" he asked.

"Nothing was said one way or the other. I suppose that since we are private they don't much care. I want to try to get a line on the people he used in LA to take care of Carolyn Clayton. I don't speak the language well enough to even know if the information was imparted to me. I don't suppose you have any state-of-the-art listening devices?" I asked.

"We can probably scare some up. How do you plan to plant them?" Nick asked.

"I don't know yet, but where there's a will, there's a way, as my grandmother used to say. There has to be a ploy we can use to gain access to his house. Whether we get the bugs in the right location is another matter, but at least we should get some indication as to his habits and the people he entertains," I said.

"Done. These guys can pick them up at our embassy. I suppose you want some way to monitor them as well?"

"That would be nice. Irvin can do all the interface. He's pretty good with electronic devices and computers," I said.

Colin said, "They will be available when you need them. John and I are taking a different flight from yours. It probably makes very little difference, but we have to play by the spy rules. Give me 24 hours after you arrive in Riyadh and call this number." He handed me a card with the number on it. The card was the exact size and shape of a regular business card but was totally blank, except for the phone number.

"I wonder where he keeps his yacht."

"Probably in dry storage. There's not a lot of places to berth them in Saudi Arabia," Nick said.

"That would be an ideal place to bug, but it would be a bitch trying to monitor the thing while he's underway," I said.

"How long do you think you will be over there?" Nick asked.

"Until we get the goods on him or Weatherly tells us the money has run out," I said.

"Well, good luck to you and if you have any needs, just let one of these two know and we will see about supplying whatever you need."

"Just out of curiosity, why was your government so willing to pay a reward for something so circumstantial?" I asked.

"Once we got the picture we went back over digital files for the time before the attacks and used facial recognition software to see if he showed up in any of our files. You know that you can't even take a piss in London without being recorded, don't you? Cameras are on every other utility pole and at all public places. You can follow someone in London all over the city without ever having to leave your desk. He was in London in May of 2005, so with what you provided to add to our own data we concluded that you were right. Having the head of DHS on your side probably helped some as well."

Chapter 13

The following day we took a flight from London directly to Riyadh, arriving in the afternoon. By the time we found a hotel it was after working hours at the Embassy so we decided to wait until morning to contact the CIA guy.

The ethnic population of the city was varied, as was the method of dress. A lot of men wore business suits, but a large number also wore traditional Arabic robes and headdress, or Keffiyeh. There were very few women who were dressed in anything except the accepted wear for women throughout the Middle East. All kept the lower parts of their faces covered. After we checked into the hotel, where we had to turn over our passports, we strolled around the business district of the city. It definitely wasn't like New York.

There were several clothing stores that we noted for future reference. The big thing that we were going to have to remember was the Islamic call to prayer. Four times per day when the call came from the many minarets scattered around the city everyone stopped what they were doing and bowed toward Mecca for prayers.

As I listened to the conversation around me some of it came back. I never was truly fluent, even in the Iraqi brand of Arabic, but I could understand enough to follow a very elementary conversation when I left three years earlier. James and I were trying to help Irvin and Sam get a handle on the more commonly used phrases.

Strangely enough, Sam picked it up really fast. He seemed to have an aptitude for languages. If he had two weeks of immersed study he would be able to pass himself off as an Arabic speaker from one of the other countries, like Somali, which used a similar language.

Irvin, on the other hand, couldn't seem to get his tongue around the words. Sam's suggestion that he play mute might have to be implemented.

We got a good night's sleep and after breakfast I called the CIA contact number that Weatherly had given me. I identified myself and asked what we were supposed to do.

"My name is Donald. Stay in your rooms and I will be there within an hour. I have pictures of you so I know what you look like," he said.

When he knocked I opened the door. He walked in with a good sized suitcase.

"If you came from the Embassy, how do you know that you weren't followed?" I asked.

"I don't operate with the rest of the company guys. I work in the administrative division and deliver suitcases to people who misplaced them on planes or even buses. I probably make at least two trips to deliver baggage each week, sometimes more. Even if they know who I really work for they would have a difficult time tying me to you guys."

He opened the suitcase on the bed. Inside were four holstered pistols wrapped up in shoulder straps. There was two boxes of ammunition for each of the weapons, two Walther PPK's and two 9 mm Berretta's. We each chose one and put them aside.

Next Donald took out a sheaf of papers held together by a large rubber band. He took the band off and spread the papers out on the bed.

"There are Somali passports for you three," he said, indicating Sam, Irvin and James. "Also work permits. The passports have entry stamps so you shouldn't run into any problems with them."

On the bottom of the suitcase were stacks of banded $100 bills, four satellite phones and a somewhat bulky package which I assumed held the listening devices and a receiver.

"Do you know how to use these?" he asked holding up one of the sat phones.

"I used them in the past but you should refresh my memory and I don't believe the other three have any experience with them," I said.

He showed us how they worked and gave us his sat phone number. "If you need to contact me that is how you will do it," he said.

"There's $5,000 in each bundle of cash. You are going to have to use cash or the pre-paid credit cards. Now, I also have a map with directions to Sarraf's home. It's sort of a compound and I will leave all that to you guys. Weatherly told me to supply whatever you need, so let me know in advance if it is something hard to come by, such as armament."

"You do know that we will be working with the Brits as well, don't you?"

"No, but it makes no difference to me. I am just the supplier," Donald said. "Having said that, if you get into trouble and need me, just call."

When we went clothes shopping the next morning my three companions decided that they were not going to wear Arabic robes. "We will just buy some work clothes," Sam said, speaking for the three of them.

I bought a couple of European cut suits and the others bought three sets of work clothes each. Levi's, long sleeved shirts, and work boots comprised the bulk of their purchases.

After we left the clothing store I said, "We need to find out where Sarraf's oil holdings are so at least one of you can apply for a job. Maybe we can get a line on how he chooses his household staff and see if we can get one of you inside," I said.

"The first thing I am going to do is buy a laptop computer. I feel naked without access to one," Irvin said.

We visited an electronics store and took care of that chore.

Next I called the number Colin had given me. He answered right away.

Colin agreed that he and John would come to our hotel that evening. "Let's make it 8:00 pm. That will give us time to have some dinner," he said.

Once we were back in my room and Colin and John showed up we got down to business.

"What's the plan?" Colin asked.

111

"There is no plan. We are going to try to get Sam hooked up with his oil business and possibly get Irvin or James on his household staff. I'm going to try to get a list of the people he does business with and watch his house to see who comes and goes. If he leaves we will try to follow him and do the same thing."

"Irvin will try to get that information for me from the computer and through local directories. If we can gain access to his house we will plant the bugs. That's when we will need you guys to translate. Perhaps we could gain entry by posing as deliverymen for some commodity. If those bugs are similar to the ones we have run across lately it will not take more than a few seconds to plant at least one," I said.

"My government has decided that it would be a good thing if he ceased to be among the living. They haven't told us to terminate him, but I believe that option is on the table," Colin said.

"At least give me enough time to try to find out who his contacts are in the states," I said.

"You know, the irony of this situation is that Sarraf doesn't see anything he has done as wrong. Their Holy Koran tells them that to wage holy war, or jihad, against infidels is perfectly acceptable. All who do not embrace Islam are considered infidels, so the world is their hunting ground," Colin said.

"Well, sometimes the prey is able to surprise the hunter. Let's hope this is one of those times. Do you have any way to get a list of numbers called on his phone for the 2005 time frame?" I asked.

"If you can come up with his cell or sat phone number I can run it by GCHQ and see if they have any luck with it. Your NSA might be able to come up with something if you work it through Weatherly," he said.

"It was just a thought. I expect both your people and ours will be doing that as a matter of routine," I said.

"I expect that you are right, now that we know the bugger we are looking for."

"Then I guess we will just stumble along and take it as it comes," I said.

"You have my number, so if you have any needs just call," Colin said.

Irvin fired up his new computer and started researching Sarraf. He found the oil company he was associated with and even managed to get the location of the drilling sites.

"We can rent a car and drive to the site. Maybe looking it over will give us some ideas," Sam suggested.

"We have to start someplace and that is just as good as any," I said.

"What do you guys say we use some of the money they provided to buy a used car? It would be much better than having to rent one," James suggested.

We all nodded affirmative. It made sense. If we had time before we left we could resell it and recoup some of the money and if not just leave it for someone to steal, of course Muslims do not steal.

Irvin continued to build a dossier on Sarraf while the rest of us practiced our Arabic.

He found that Sarraf had three sons and a daughter. The ages were from 14 down. The girl was the eldest and the youngest son was only two. The others were four and eight.

The wife was of no significance since they only showed their eyes when in public.

Sarraf didn't have an office. He apparently used his home for that purpose when he needed to have a face to face meeting with someone.

We all turned in at around 10:00 pm.

The next morning we went in search of a car. Saudi Arabia didn't seem to have many used car lots. Most people we learned placed advertisements in various papers and places when they wanted to sell something of value.

I picked up a couple of papers and we managed to find a couple of ads that we could decipher that related to automobiles for sale. One was a 2004 Mercedes, the smaller variant, or 200 series in today's lingo.

I copied the address and phone number and we took a taxi to within walking distance of the address.

"I think it would be better if I make the approach," I said. "I can pose as an American who came to work in the oil industry as a means of disguising my lack of Arabic knowledge."

"Do you want to take the money with you?" James asked.

"I don't think so. That would raise a red flag by walking around with that kind of money on my person. If I can cut a deal I will tell him that I have to visit a bank and offer him either American or their currency," I said.

Sam and the other two found a restaurant and would wait for me there. I found the house, which turned out to be a walled villa with a guard at the entrance.

I approached him and explained that I wanted to look at the car for sale. I told him I worked in the oil business.

He used his cell phone to call inside the house and soon a man came out and asked how he could help.

"I'm sorry but I don't speak your language. I am from America and came over to work in the oil industry. I am in need of a used car that can take the rugged terrain. I was told that you have an older model for sale."

"I have a Mercedes 210 of the year 2004. It is in good condition. I can show it to you," he said, motioning for me to enter the grounds.

We went to the garage, which housed four cars. The older one was flanked by a 2008 of the same series and two newer larger ones.

He popped the hood latch and we looked at the engine. He then started it up and it ran very smoothly.

"What is your asking price?" I asked.

"I will give you a good deal. Only $15,000, if you are paying in dollars," he said.

"Sorry, that's much more than I can afford. I was thinking about something half that price," I said.

"You will not find anything that inexpensive unless it is older and unreliable. I will, against my better judgement, let you have it for $12,000."

"I will give you $10,000. To do that I will have to eat roots and berries for months," I said.

He looked at me appraisingly. "You may not speak the language, but you know our bartering methods. I will sell it to you for $10,000."

"I will visit the bank and be back later. How will we handle the title transfer?"

"When you return with the money, you and I will visit the vehicle office and change the title. There is a pretty hefty fee for that, something like five percent of the sale price. I can help a bit there by listing the sale price a couple of thousand less than you agreed to pay," he said.

"You are very kind," I said. "I will return in about one hour."

I joined the others at the restaurant and we ate more cheese and fruit and killed the hour.

I got $3,000 from each of them and went back to the owner's house.

I drove the 2004 and he drove one of the newer models to the motor vehicle office and we processed the paperwork. I paid just under $2,400 for the registration and got the new tag. We then parted ways.

I registered the car in my own name and provided my California driver's license for identification.

I picked up the others and we went back to the hotel.

"See if can get a line on his oil holdings so we will know where to go," I said to Irvin.

"I'm on it," he said.

The rest of us didn't have much to do so we lounged around while Irvin was on the computer.

I somehow fell asleep on the couch.

When I awoke, after about 15 minutes, Sam was talking to Matt on his sat phone.

"Ask him to go through Carolyn's belongings and look for tag numbers jotted down on anything. The most obvious places would be in her purses if she had multiple ones. Have him check her desk contents and see if that yields anything as well," I said.

Sam relayed the message.

"He says that the cops caught Trevor in the act. He is now in jail, and the cigarettes came from a warehouse heist and they tied the one who delivered them to a gang. Looks like that is going to turn out all right," Sam said.

"Wish I could say the same for our job," I said.

I was frustrated. I just didn't see a way to find out what we needed to know without access to Sarraf.

If Matt could come up with tag numbers it is possible that the ones who abducted Carolyn used their own cars. That would be nice, but was probably wishful thinking.

Irvin finally said, "I think I have his oil field located. It's a long way from here if I have the right one."

"Which direction?" I asked.

"East, or maybe south east."

"What's the distance?"

"I would guess from the map scale about 150 miles."

"We will have breakfast in the morning and then see if we can locate it. In the meantime let's so see how old Abdul is doing at home."

We drove to the outskirts of the city, which was no easy chore not knowing the roads and having no navigation system in the car.

Irvin used his sat phone to call up the navigation app and fed me directions. We made some false turns when the streets became one way against us but finally found the house.

We knew from the satellite pictures on google earth that the house was inside a compound protected by a wall that was around 10 feet tall. Nothing could be seen from the outside but the gate, which was guarded by a rifle wielding sentry.

I drove around looking for someplace inconspicuous to park but didn't find anything that would escape the attention of the guard and still provide a view of the entrance to the compound.

Finally I just parked on the next street over and we walked around the area. There was no location that provided a view inside the compound unless we could get access to one of the houses in the area with at least two, preferably three stories.

Even then we would not have an unobstructed view of the entire inside of the compound.

We certainly couldn't afford to purchase one of the houses, though if we could justify it the CIA might buy it. I didn't even want to go there.

It was obvious that we were going to have to somehow gain access to the grounds through legitimate means. That meant that one of us would have to pose as a delivery man, or gain employment somehow. The prospects didn't look promising.

After a couple of circuits around the block we returned to the hotel, had supper and went to bed early.

Chapter 14

While I slept that night I either had a very vivid dream, or a visit from Carolyn. I saw her at the foot of my bed and she uttered a single name. I don't know how, but I even knew the proper spelling. I didn't wake when it happened, so I can't put it into the proper perspective. I just knew that it had been Carolyn.

When we all got together that morning I told the others about it.

"What was the name?" Sam asked.

"Usha Bin Dahari. The spelling is correct I think because that is what stuck with me. Going by what Lillian told us, the name has some connection to Carolyn's death. I don't know if it is a name to look into over here, or back in the states," I said.

"Why don't you pass the name to Matt and see if he can get a line on anyone by that name back in L.A.?" Irvin asked.

"Might as well look at both locations since I have no idea what the name means."

If we had called then it would have been the middle of the night in L.A., so we waited until afternoon. By then we were well on our way to Sarraf's oil holdings. This time we had acquired maps off the internet and printed them out. Irvin used a tourist web site so the names would be in English as well as Arabic.

I told Matt to keep the name in mind while going through Carolyn's belongings.

Since the ploy was to get Sam a job in the oil field he had packed his suitcase with the work clothing and his toilet articles. I called Matt while we were on the road and gave him the name. "Anything you can find on that name will be helpful," I said.

"I'm going to start going through her belongings tomorrow," Matt said. "I talked to the Clayton's today and they gave me the okay."

The location we were looking for was in the direction of the Saudi border with Iraq but short of it. The roads were not like interstate highways back home but were in a pretty good state of repair. Once outside the city the traffic was nothing like what we were used to even on state highways at home.

We saw more pack animals than cars it seemed, and they were not shy about using their portion of the road and yours too if they had more than one animal.

Going was slow for that reason and it took us almost six hours to travel the 150 miles. That included a stop for cheese, fruit and bread at a wayside restaurant.

The Saudi's were happy to take dollars and we had no trouble in that regard. As we neared the area Irvin had pinpointed oil wells could be seen across the landscape. It was kind of like the deserts of California in the San Joaquin Valley, or in west Texas. Some producing well heads were pumping, while others sat dormant.

"Do you know anything at all about the oil business?" I asked Sam.

"I know it is pumped out of the ground and ultimately powers my car, but other than that I'm lost."

I provided a quick tutorial based on my knowledge of the process. "First of all it doesn't come out of the ground in geysers like the movies portrayed in some of the flicks. It is mixed with water and other minerals when it is pumped. It looks almost like watery puke to me. That has to be refined, which means taking the oil out of the mixture that originally came out of the ground. I know very little about the process, but I do know that the residue is very salty. Back home they have been reinjecting the residue below the level where the oil was pumped from. That serves two purposes. It gets rid of the slag that they would otherwise have to get rid of in some other way, and it forces more oil to the well head. They drill horizontally to keep from having to drill new wells from scratch. There has been a lot of controversy over the reinjection of the residue. It apparently causes earthquakes. Now you are an expert," I said.

"I imagine if they hire me it will be to do the heavy lifting," he said.

We asked directions to the company offices and it took half a dozen tries before we found someone who could give us directions.

Even then it was not an easy task. We drove for almost an hour trying to locate the office.

When we did find it I was not very impressed. It looked as if they had taken two double-wide mobile homes and mated them. The equipment storage facilities were co-located and their facilities were much larger than the offices. They apparently maintained their own equipment because there was a lot of it near the entrance to the work bays in various states of disassembly.

Sam went to the office and the rest of us waited outside.

He was inside for more than half an hour, and when he came out he had a wide grin on his face.

"I take it things went well," I said.

"You are looking at the newest employee of the Sarraf Oil Company. Apparently there's a lot of heavy lifting that has to be done. One look at my size and they would have hired me if I had leprosy," Sam said.

"When do you start?"

"Tomorrow. They have a barracks for the oil field workers but I don't know if that will work for me or not. I had enough of the smelly locker rooms during my football days. I will reserve judgement until I look the situation over. The pay is $250 per day."

"Where is this barracks located?"

Sam handed me a map with the location. I handed it to Irvin. "Think you can find this?" I asked.

"One way or another. There's always the satellite map if I need help."

We climbed back into the car and went in search of Sam's new home.

"Call me at least daily," I said. "If you find out anything worthwhile call immediately."

Sam could get by with English in the oil fields, but Irvin and James would not be able to do so as household staff. I had about given up on that the second day in Saudi Arabia.

120

John Buckner

"It looks like we three are going to do the surveillance on Sarraf," I said after Sam took his bag into the barracks and we were on our way back to Riyadh.

"If he goes anywhere in his car maybe we can get access long enough to plant one of the bugs in his car," Irvin said.

"I think just knowing who visits him, and who he visits will tell us a lot. From his actions with the London bomber I don't believe he will use the telephone for important discussions, at least of the type we are interested in," I said.

"How long are we going to spend on this?"

"If we don't have something in two weeks I will call Weatherly and tell him it doesn't look promising," I said.

We would take turns watching Sarraf's house. The hours of darkness I didn't worry too much about. I didn't believe he was stupid enough to have terrorists come to his home, then again he would not be worried about any surveillance at home, and so my assumption might be incorrect.

When we arrived back at our hotel it was already late evening so we had dinner and went to bed. We were ready to start the surveillance the following day and I thought it might be a good idea to have a good quality camera so we could get good pictures if the opportunity presented itself.

We made a run to the same electronics store where Irvin had purchased the lap top. I parted with nearly $500 to get a decent camera. It had a fantastic zoom feature. At the very least we could get license plate numbers to pass on to the Brits and the CIA.

The plan was to use the car for the surveillance, but one of us would be in the neighborhood on foot part of the time. Parking on the street in a residential neighborhood was not the best way to do the watching and even being on foot for long periods would seem suspicious to those who lived there.

However, it was the best I could come up with, short of buying one of the houses across the street, and that wasn't going to happen.

I had on my pessimist hat today and I just didn't think the surveillance would turn up anything usable.

Irvin and I took the first shift. We found a parking place where we could see the entrance to Sarraf's property and watched for most of the morning. Nobody came to the property during that time, nor did anyone leave.

We took a break for lunch at a nearby restaurant and when we went back Irvin stayed in the car and I strolled around the neighborhood for an hour.

A delivery van showed up in the afternoon and that was the only action we saw.

We went back to the hotel and James took the car and headed back to the stakeout.

We continued for a week without anything of significance happening. We rotated shifts and it was during the evening of the eighth day that Sarraf finally left his house.

Irvin and I followed the car into the main part of town. Sarraf was alone, save for the chauffeur and went to a restaurant in one of the major hotels. I drove on for a block and entered a parking garage. Irvin and I then walked back to the hotel. We entered separately and I spotted Sarraf sitting alone at a table in the restaurant. The restaurant had glass separating it from the lobby of the hotel and we could keep an eye on him from different points in the lobby.

Irvin found a chair with a view and I browsed among the shops in the lobby. It wasn't long before Sarraf was joined by another man. The newcomer looked very young compared to Sarraf. I guessed his age to be early to mid-twenties. He was in casual western dress. He had on jeans and a polo shirt. He had a scraggly beard and wore a keffiyeh, which to me looked strange with the western clothing.

I started searching for an angle to get a picture when they finished their lunch.

I checked to make sure the flash feature of the camera was turned off and experimented with the zoom from across the lobby. I could pull them in pretty tight but I had no idea what effect the glass would have on the photo. I snapped a couple anyway and moved to a different location.

They were in the restaurant for almost an hour and when they got up to leave I gave Irvin the high sign and moved toward the main entrance to get a good angle. I kept the camera up to my eye, watching the restaurant entrance through the viewfinder.

The second they walked out and turned toward me I took the picture. They were in conversation and didn't seem to notice. I motioned to James and we walked outside.

"I want to follow the younger one and see if he will lead us to anyone. We can pick up Sarraf later," I said.

I followed the new man on foot while Irvin went to retrieve the car. All Irvin knew was our direction. If the man turned I would need to let Irvin know by phone.

The phone call was not required as the man kept on a straight path. I was about half a block behind him when Irvin pulled alongside and honked the horn lightly. I motioned for him to circle the block.

A couple of blocks farther and he entered a mosque. I waited for Irvin's next circuit and motioned him to the curb. I got in and told him where the man had gone.

"I want to try to pick him up when he leaves. Find a place to park and we will both watch on foot. When he comes out one of us can follow while the other retrieves the car."

The wait this time was longer. He was inside for longer than an hour. If he was saying his prayers he must have had a load of things to say to the prophet.

He was not alone when he came out. There were two others with him, dressed as he was, except one didn't have a keffiyeh. I was half a block away but the camera zoomed in so the picture looked like close-up.

Shortly a cab pulled to the curb and the three got in.

We were parked far enough from where we were now that there was no chance of picking them up again.

We went back to the hotel and Irvin transferred the pictures to the computer.

Irvin said, "Not bad for an amateur. The shot from the lobby and the one at the mosque are pretty good."

I told James, "Let's skip the surveillance for the remainder of the day. I think he just met with some more of the bad guys."

I called the number Colin had given me and asked if he could come to the hotel.

I did the same for the CIA contact. I wanted to get the pictures to Weatherly and I didn't have an e-mail address for him.

Donald arrived first, followed by Colin and John about ten minutes later.

I had Irvin pull up the pictures on the computer.

"Today is the first time he has left his house in more than a week. The chauffeur drove him to the business section and he went into a hotel restaurant. He was met by the man in the picture with him. We decided to follow the new guy and he walked several blocks. I followed on foot and Irvin retrieved our car and circled the block until the man went into a mosque. We parked the car about a block away and went back to the area of the mosque and waited. When he came out about 90 minutes later he was with these two," I said, pointing to the new image Irvin had called up. They got into a cab and we were stuck high and dry due to the distance to our car."

They all looked closely at the two pictures.

"I think I might recognize one of those guys," Colin said.

"I want to get these to our people back at CIA. You can download the pictures from the camera to get to your people," I said to Colin. "I need an e-mail address to send them to Weatherly."

Colin took the chip from the camera and uploaded the pictures to his sat phone. Donald said he didn't have an e-mail address for Weatherly but suggested that I do the same thing Colin was doing. "Upload the pictures to your sat phone and send them that way. It will be faster and I don't think the bad guys have much of a SIGINT effort going."

I had watched Colin and still had to get help loading them into the phone.

"Where's the big bloke?" Colin asked, referring to Sam.

"We got him a job in Sarraf's oil field. He has been there for more than a week. He calls in each day and so far hasn't uncovered anything worthwhile."

I had a wild thought and asked the group, "Have any of you ever come across the name Usha Bin Dahari?"

All shook their heads negative.

"Does the name have meaning?" Colin asked.

"I had a visit from our missing person. She said the name and faded away. It has to have something to do with Sarraf or she wouldn't have provided the name," I replied.

"You actually saw her well enough to recognize her?"

"Just as clear as looking at you," I said, reaching near him and patting an imaginary figure on the back.

Irvin almost fell out of his chair laughing. It took the others a minute to figure out what caused the fit of laughter, then everyone joined him.

"No, seriously, she was as clear as a picture and said the name. She then just disappeared."

I sent the message to Weatherly, attaching the photo's to the file. I only said, "Hope these are useful," in the text message.

When Sam called the next day I asked if he was ready to go home.

"Give me a couple of more days. I think I might be able to find out something. Some of the guys were talking last night about terrorist attacks. They were speaking Somali and I didn't get much of it, but I think they might know something," Sam said.

"Okay, two more days."

I told the others that Sam might have a lead and we were going to stay for a couple of more days.

"We can watch Sarraf for those two days," I said.

When Sam called late the next day he had some news. "One of the Somali's had an accident. Some piping rolled off a lift and pinned him underneath. I lifted the pipes and freed him. He had a broken leg and while everyone else was standing around watching I found a couple of pieces of light packing wood and made a splint for his obviously broken leg. We got him back to the barracks and everyone else went back to work. I stayed with

125

him and we talked some. He's only 18 years old and regrets having left home to work for the Saudi's. He said that six of them had been recruited for a holy mission and though he wasn't even very religious he saw it as a way to get out of Somalia where conditions are horrid even compared to the way we were living here."

"He said that Sarraf is the money behind a number of terrorist cells. He then told me that he thought I was there to find out about them."

"I didn't lie to the kid, but told him that we were looking at Sarraf because he had killed a very young woman simply because she had seen him with the guy who bombed the London subway."

"Did he have any specifics on the mission they were to undertake?"

"No, but he said he thought it would be in the United States," Sam replied.

"Find out if he is interested in going to the USA. I think we can talk the CIA into putting him into their protection program. I will discuss it with Weatherly and let you know tomorrow," I said.

I then called Weatherly, even though it would be the middle of the night in Washington. He answered on the third ring and in a sleepy voice said, "Hello."

I said, "This is Brad. I have a person I think you would be interested in talking with. Any chance of putting him into your protection program?"

"You do know this is an unsecure line?"

"Yes, and I also know that the terrorists don't have much of a SIGIINT capability. Just give me a yes or no."

"Does he know enough to be of any use?"

"Would a planned attack on the U.S. be enough?"

That got his attention.

"Did he tell you this?"

"No, he told Sam."

"Does this have to be done right now?"

"Not at this very minute, but I believe the informant is in danger. He had some pipes fall on him and broke his leg. Sam got him out and splinted the leg. The others just went back to work as if nothing had happened. I think that made our boy see just how ruthless and uncaring they are. He also told Sam that he thought he was there to spy on Sarraf. If he thinks that, then the others might as well. I think it is time to pull up stakes. On another subject, did the pictures I sent help any?"

"We got a hit on two of the ones in front of the mosque. They are known terrorists."

"Is the answer to the other problem yes, or no?"

"Get him someplace where you can protect him until I can set things up. I will call you tomorrow, probably late in the day."

I called Sam back, not knowing if he would answer or not. It took five rings but he finally answered. I didn't waste time on preliminaries but said, "Get him out of there if you can. Call and let me know where to meet you. We will leave right now and Irvin will have the satellite map. We know the location of the barracks so give us a direction and distance from there," I said.

"You mean tonight?"

"Are you sure the accident was that and not a way to get rid of a weak link?" I asked.

"Now that you mention it, it could have been planned."

"I will try to get him into one of the jeeps and once I choose a direction I will call and let you know."

"Okay, the rest of us are leaving now."

We packed our meager luggage and checked out of the hotel, not forgetting to retrieve our passports.

While Irvin and I were checking out, James visited a kiosk and stocked up on water and junk food. It was going to be a long night.

We drove for almost three hours before we heard from Sam. "I had to convince him that it was the right thing to do. I told him the accident was not an accident but had been planned by his fellow workers to get rid of him."

"I think what convinced him was that the others when they came in from work just treated him like he wasn't there. I waited until everyone was asleep and carried him down to one of the company jeeps. We are now at least ten miles from the barracks on a northerly heading. Do you want me to wait here or continue to drive?"

"Are you safe where you are?"

"I believe so. In any event I still have the pistol and they are not likely to send out a search party until daylight."

"Okay we will try to find you where you are now. If you have to move let us know."

It took another half hour to find Sam and the informant.

When we did, Sam made the introductions. The Somali could speak some English. That was one of the prerequisites for being chosen for the mission.

"Did they tell you it would be a suicide mission?" I asked.

"No they simply told us that we would be briefed when the time was right, but they did tell us that the mission would take place in Los Angeles, California. Isn't that where Disneyland is located?"

"Close enough," Sam said.

"You do want to go to the United States don't you?" I asked just to be sure we would not have to take him kicking and dragging.

"Oh yes sir, more than anything," he said with tears in his eyes.

"How old are you?" I asked.

"I am 18, but I look older," he said.

Well, I thought, at least we won't be abducting a minor.

We had been headed back in the general direction of Riyadh and I wasn't sure that was a good idea.

"Let's stop someplace for a while until we find out what Weatherly has in mind. He might want us to go someplace else to make it easier to get us out."

We found a Wadi and James pulled the vehicle off the road and behind some brush. We all got out and stretched our legs. Even Hakim, our defector, managed to hobble around a bit.

We had driven the jeep Sam had stolen into the brush, hopefully it would not be discovered right away.

The sun was pretty hot and I moved the car around to take advantage of what little shade there was. We finished the last of the water around noon and I decided that we had better get on the way, to hell with what Weatherly wanted. We needed water and food and the road to Riyadh provided the closest source of both.

While we were enroute my sat phone rang. It was Weatherly.

"Can you get to the Iraq border?"

"That's a pretty long border. What particular stretch do you want us at?"

"Just past where Kuwait, Iraq and Saudi Arabia come together. I will have a helicopter there by the time you arrive and I will give you his sat phone number so you can let him know exactly where you are."

"Okay, but it's a long way from where we are right now. It will take us six or seven hours to get there."

"How are you travelling?"

"In a used Mercedes I bought the day after we got here. I used the money you provided through Donald. I am probably going to have to just leave it when we join up with the helicopter."

"That's no big deal. Just sign the title and someone will find it in a day or two."

Irvin plotted us a new route, but before we got off on the back roads I wanted to eat and stock up on junk food.

We found a small roadside restaurant in an obscure town and went in. We all ate our fill and purchased a case of drinking water.

We took turns driving, except for Irvin. He was our navigator and kept a constant eye on the map.

It was late in the evening and we were still over a hundred miles from our intended destination. My phone rang and it was Weatherly.

"Take down this number," he said.

I mimed a writing instrument and Irvin handed me a pen and notepad.

"Okay, ready."

He read the number off and I repeated it back to make sure I had it down correctly.

"When you get to the area of the Kuwait/Iraq border give them a call on that number. Once you are on the helicopter they will know what to do. One of my people will be with them."

"We're still almost 100 miles away, so tell them not to expect a call right away."

"Understand. I will relay your message," he said and hung up.

Irvin got us to a road that paralleled the border and we simply kept driving until he could determine that we were in the vicinity of the Kuwait border. I then called the number I had been given and got the pilot on the phone.

"We are in the vicinity of the Kuwait border. What now?" I asked.

"Are you on the main road?"

"Yes, I think so."

"I should be within ten miles of your location. The Saudi's have border patrols and I will need to dodge them. Is there much traffic on the road?"

"Very little. Just stay on the road and keep it at 40 MPH. I should be able to locate you with my radar."

After they hung up I told James, who was driving, to hold it at 40 MPH.

We drove several more miles before we heard the distinctive sound of a helicopter. The noise was apparently baffled because he was almost on us before we heard the sound of the prop blades. James pulled the car off the road and we all go out, Sam helping Hakim.

The helicopter landed in the road and we all piled in.

It was obviously Hakim's first ride on a helicopter because he appeared very nervous. In a very few minutes we were in Iraq. The chopper continued toward Baghdad but landed well short of that well known area at a desolate U.S. base.

Once we were on the ground the CIA man took us to a rather large tent, which turned out to be a mess hall, and asked if we were hungry.

Sam, of course, never turns down the offer of food so we all ate.

While we were eating the CIA rep told us that we would be taken to Balad air force base where we would be processed for travel to the U.S.

While we were there I asked if a medic could look at Hakim's leg. Sam accompanied him to the dispensary and they came back in about an hour with Hakim's leg encased in a plaster cast and using a pair of crutches.

Eventually we were loaded onto another helicopter and taken to a large air base. Papers were made up for Hakim and later that night we boarded a military transport for Germany.

The plane had hardly finished its landing roll when someone in civilian clothing came aboard and asked us to follow him. He took us to a small office, sat down before a computer and asked Hakim his full name, age, and date of birth. He also asked him where he was born.

With all the information entered he printed out a form that was apparently an immigration permit. We would need that to get through customs when we got to the states.

When Hakim looked at the entry visa tears ran unashamedly down his cheeks.

We stayed at the airport until someone told us to follow them and we boarded another cargo plane, this one configured for passengers, though we were the only passengers on board.

Once the preliminaries were over the pilot took off. Within half an hour Hakim exclaimed excitedly, there's the ocean.

We all laughed.

"It's in the same old place as always, Hakim," Sam said.

I decided that I was going to get as much out of Hakim as I could before turning him over to the CIA.

Once we reached cruising altitude I started asking questions. Irvin, I noticed, was taking notes on his laptop.

"Tell me about how they recruited you," I said.

"They came to my village and asked if anyone could speak English. I had been studying very hard because I wanted to come to America for a long time, so I raised my hand. One of them, there were three, asked me some questions in English and he was satisfied that I could speak enough for his purposes."

"They took me aside and asked about my religion. If I had been dumb enough to say anything other than Islam they would not have taken me. I still didn't know what they wanted English speaking people for, so I asked."

"You were chosen by Allah to be a part of a group who will deal a great blow to the infidels," he said.

"Will I go to England?"

"No but even better, to America. You might even be able to go to Disneyland before your mission commences. We will take you to Saudi Arabia. There you will be employed in the oil fields until the mission plan is finished. You will be provided food and a place to sleep as well as being paid a good wage for the work you do."

"Is Disneyland in Los Angeles?" I asked.

"Close enough," he said.

"We joined up with five others, plus the recruiters, and took a boat to Saudi Arabia. We were then trucked to the oil field. Before you came Mister Sam, we had training with rifles and pistols. We did this right there in the oil field."

"Did they give you any indication as to your target?" I asked.

"No but it wouldn't surprise me if it didn't turn out to be Disneyland. The recruiter seemed to be thrown off by my mention of the place."

"Did you see any others while you were in the oil field?"

"One evening two men came to us and talked in English. I think they were just making sure that we really could speak the language before giving us any additional information."

"Irvin," I said, "fire up your laptop and see if Hakim recognizes either of the three from the mosque."

When he had the picture on the screen I showed it to Hakim. He looked and nodded affirmative. "Those are two who came to the barracks."

"Did they ask any specific questions, or just enough to see if you really could speak English?"

"They talked about what a glorious day it would be and how we were going to take the lives of more people than any of our other groups ever had, with the exception of the twin towers attacks."

"They still didn't give you any indication as to the location?"

"Only that we would need to go to Los Angeles."

"Did they give any indication as to when?"

"No, but I got the impression that it would not be very far in the future," Hakim said.

"You didn't get any training about how to make explosives?" I asked.

"No. They just said we were adequate to the task."

"You had no idea that they planned to use you as a suicide bomber?"

"If I had I certainly would not have come, or if they had told me after we got here I would have run away. I do not have a death wish. This life is the only one I have and I don't want to give it up for some religious reason, especially when I don't believe in their religion."

"What did they tell the other people in your village about taking you away?"

"I don't know, but I did see them passing money to the headman of my village."

"Did you hear the name Usha Bin Dahari mentioned?"

"No, but I did hear them talking among themselves and the name Usha was mentioned by one of them."

I looked at Sam and the others. "I think that Usha is already in the states, possibly legally so, and will build the bombs. These guys were supposed to show up and strap on the explosives and he would deliver them to Disneyland. Another scenario is that they have someone on the inside at Disneyland who will take the explosives over the fence and outfit them when they show up."

What we had learned was above and beyond what I thought we would come up with when this little escapade started. I believe we now have a link to Carolyn's killer(s) in the form of Usha Bin Dahari. He may not be in the phone book but I felt sure he lived in the Los Angeles area.

Chapter 15

We all slept a good portion of the flight back to McGuire air force base in New Jersey.

We were met by two men in Civilian clothes and after getting our passports stamped the two accompanied Hakim to immigration control and cleared him.

We then boarded a small business jet and flew to Andrews air force base and transferred to one of the large SUV's.

I didn't pay much attention to our direction of travel because it was of no concern to me.

Weatherly met us when we arrived at a secluded farm house in either the Virginia or Maryland countryside. We all went inside and gathered around a large dining table. A recorder was set up in the middle of the table.

Weatherly first of all welcomed Hakim to the United States and told him that his agency would protect him.

The questions then started. They were much more thorough than my talk with Hakim.

Hakim positively identified the two who had been at the barracks and was able to identify another from pictures they showed him.

Try as they might to get him to reveal the time and date of the planned attack Hakim could not give them information he did not possess. About the best he could do was to convince them that what he had seen in the eyes of his recruiter when he mentioned Disneyland indeed pointed to that as the target.

When we took a break after almost three hours, Weatherly got me aside and told me he was very pleased with what we had uncovered. "I will send the payment via FEDEX with receipt required. It will be in cash, so how you handle the taxes are your concern."

"I might need some help in Los Angles from someone who knows the area. May I call on you if needed?" he added.

"Of course. I am going to try to get a line on Usha Bin Dahari. I believe he is responsible for Carolyn Clayton's death. I won't throw a monkey wrench into your affairs, but I might have additional information that would be helpful to you when you start to work the problem from our area," I said.

"I will keep in touch by phone," he said.

"How do we get back to California?" I asked.

"I will have someone drive you to the airport. BWI is closest if that's all right with you."

"That will work. If I can help in any way, just let me know."

They shook hands and left for the airport after saying goodbye to Hakim.

"Will I see you again?" he asked.

Sam gave him a business card and told him to call at any time.

We got into L.A. late and called Matt to come pick us up.

On the way back to the house I asked him if he had found anything in Carolyn's belongings.

"No. There was some papers in one of her purses but I didn't see anything that looked like what you told me to look for. You might want to go through them again yourself," he said.

"I need to brief the Clayton's anyway. We can do that tomorrow," I said.

"Weatherly didn't say anything about the money we have left. I suggest we just keep it," I said.

"Works for me," Sam replied. "I didn't even get my check for the work in the oil field."

"Well at least you are still getting paid by the CIA. Weatherly told me he was sending the cash by FEDEX. That's going to amount to several thousand dollars. With the reward from the Brits we did pretty well on this case so far," I said.

"It was a stroke of luck finding Hakim," Sam said.

Matt, of course, didn't know what he was talking about so Sam told him the entire story.

"That really was luck. What will the CIA do with him after they get all they can out of him?" Matt asked.

"I don't know. Probably keep him safe someplace until all this plays out. I believe the British will take care of Sarraf in their own way," Sam said.

"What did you do with the bugs?" I asked Irvin.

"They're in my suitcase. We might have a use for them one of these days. I will play with them a bit and see how sensitive they are. I think the CIA just wrote everything off when they gave it to us," he replied.

We were jet-lagged and turned in after the conversation with Matt.

I was up early the next morning. I sat down at my computer to document all we had found out so far. I don't know why but sometimes when I do that I will stumble onto something that I hadn't caught while the events were taking place.

The question that nagged me was why they would choose Disneyland for the attack. Sure they would kill a lot of people with half a dozen suicide bombers at various locations throughout the park, but if they were trying to send a message, what was the message.

I mean, an attack on an amusement park didn't strike me as a very sophisticated way to undermine a country's political views. If Disneyland was really their target and they managed to kill a lot of people, it would only cause us to put more effort into rooting out terrorists.

Possibly they wanted to send a message that Americans were not even safe in their own country.

Whatever the reason, Hakim felt pretty certain that the target was Disneyland.

The recruits were told that they didn't need any expertise in bomb making, so that meant that someone locally was going to prepare the packages, and that led me back to Usha Bin Dahari. We did not run across the name in Saudi Arabia, so he must be here, otherwise Carolyn would not have passed his name to me.

My main objective was to bring Carolyn's killers to justice and the best way to do that was to find Usha Bin Dahari.

I had made a pot of coffee and the others came awake to the smell of it brewing.

I finished my narrative on the computer and moved into the kitchen for coffee and some cereal.

I asked matt, "How did the police collar Trevor and his accomplice?"

He laughed. "The same way we found out what was going on. They posted a man in the attic with a radio and when the accomplice showed up he called in the troops. Mr. Lambert, the store owner was overjoyed with the outcome. He called me the next day and we met for breakfast. He handed me a check for $5,000. It's on the counter over there."

"We got a check from the British government for £100,000. That equates to just over $130,000 in our money. Looks as if we will be solvent for a good while," I said.

"The really great thing about it is that we are so busy making money we don't have time to spend it," Sam said.

We all laughed.

"I'm going to leave the money from the British in our operating fund. When Weatherly sends the cash we will divide it five ways. If my calculations are correct we should each get about $15, 000," I said.

"In the meantime, there are several possible cases that came in while you guys were out gallivanting around the Middle East. I called all of them back and told them that if their problems could wait we would get back to them. At least three said they would wait to hear from us. I don't believe any of them were in a real hurry," Matt said.

"I'll start returning calls this afternoon. Right now Sam and I are going to the Clayton's, and then to Lillian's."

I called the Clayton's and told them we would come out this morning if it was convenient.

We arrived at 9:30 and Roberta had coffee and breakfast rolls set out. We gathered around the dining room table and I related the events in Saudi Arabia and how we had tied Sarraf to terrorism.

"I got the name of someone connected with the case that I believe is here in Los Angeles. Once we can locate him I think he will lead us to others. I believe he was the one who actually had the job of dealing with Carolyn. As far as Sarraf, the guy who ordered Carolyn's death, I believe the British are going to take care of him."

I told them about Hakim and the help he had been to us and that he identified two more people who were in on the plot to commit a terrorist act here in the states. "He is from Somalia and is very bright. He is only 18 but looks older. I think the CIA will keep him under wraps until they get a handle on the terrorist plot."

"What kind of skills does he have?" Harry asked.

"I don't think he has any that would do him any good here, other than manual labor jobs."

"You are sure he is honest?"

"Yes sir. He told us that he only went along with the recruiters as a way to leave Somalia. He took a liking to Sam, who had gotten a job in the oil field owned by Sarraf, and told him about the plot. I called Weatherly from the CIA and he arranged to get us out by helicopter. He's very personable and shouldn't have any trouble once the CIA turns him loose."

"I might be able to use him to do the outside work here. There's a small apartment out back where he might be able to live," Harry said.

"We will keep that in mind," I said. "Sam and I want to go through Carolyn's stuff again. Matt said he didn't find anything, but I believe there has to be at least one license plate number written down somewhere in her belongings."

Harry took us to the garage where Carolyn's goods were stored and we got to work.

After an hour, in which we didn't find anything, I said, "Pull all the drawers out of the tables and chest."

When Sam pulled out the drawer to one of her nightstands we hit pay dirt. At the bottom of the night stand was a business card. I looked it over. It was one of Carolyn's own cards and on the back was a license plate number.

Harry had been watching and talking to us as we went through everything.

I showed him the number. "I believe this is the plate number of whoever was following her shortly before she disappeared. I will have the Westlake police department run it and see if we can get an identity of the owner. I think it will probably be a personal car owned by one of her abductors. They would not take a chance on stealing a car for the surveillance job. I don't think they are that sophisticated," I said.

Instead of going to the Westlake P.D. I called Eddie Sanchez and asked him to run the plate. He did it while I waited.

"The name on the registration is Usha Bin Dahari," he said.

"What's the address?" I asked.

"It's in Ontario." He gave me the address and I copied it down.

After I hung up I said to Sam, "Well, there's our connection to Dahari."

"Proof once again that the spirits don't lie," Sam said in the imitation of a voice from Outer Limits.

"Okay, Matt and Larry can have the first watch. You and James can relieve them. If he is much of a night person, Irvin and I will form the third team."

We stopped by Lillian's and brought her up to date. I told her about my encounter with Carolyn and the name she gave me. "We just connected the name to those who were following her before the abduction."

I told them about our adventures in Saudi Arabia and how we had verified Sarraf's connection to terrorist groups.

"So how are they going to deal with him?" Merle asked.

"We worked with a couple of British Intelligence guys over there and they indicated that assassination was not out of the question. My money would be on his having a fatal accident sometime in the near future," I said.

"Are they sure he was behind the bombings in London?"

"After we identified him for them they ran a facial recognition and found that he was in London a couple of months before the bombings. They were sure enough to pay us the reward for identifying him for them. They really wanted this guy and have been searching for five years without a sniff," I said.

"So what are you going to do about Dahari?" Lillian asked.

"Follow him everywhere he goes until the FEDS call us off. I think they are waiting for the guys from Saudi Arabia to show up entering the country."

"You think Dahari is the contact man?" Merle asked.

"I don't see how it could be otherwise. There are probably others, and among them has to be at least one who can make bombs."

"Do the FEDS know about Dahari?"

"Probably not. I mentioned the name but I don't know if they took me seriously. We will follow him and try to get pictures of everyone he has contact with."

When we left Lillian's we went straight back to the house. I told Irvin that we now had confirmation about Dahari and had his address. "See if you can find the address on the satellite map so we can get an idea about how the house is laid out."

It didn't take long. Irvin showed us the map and zoomed in on the house in question. It was a ranch and had a wall surrounding it. We couldn't get the resolution fine enough to see what it was made of, but it didn't matter anyway.

"I want Matt and Larry to take the first watch. Try to find some inconspicuous place to watch the house. Follow him everywhere he goes."

"Why don't we install a camera on one of the power poles like the mafia did to us? Then we don't need to worry so much about the neighbors becoming suspicious about strangers hanging around the neighborhood," Irvin said.

"You think you can climb a utility pole?" Sam asked. "I'm sure not going to try it."

"We could rent a truck from someplace like Home Depot and a scissor lift from an equipment company. We could then park under the pole and raise the lift while it sits on the trailer. Shouldn't take more than a few minutes to get the job done. We will need to do it while he is not home though," Irvin said.

"Okay, head on down to the electronics store and get what you need," I said. "Sam and I will go rent the truck and lift. Matt, you and Larry go ahead and start watching the place. We can't take any action until we are sure he is not at home."

We all left to our individual assignments.

Matt called in the late afternoon to inform me that Dahari had just left his house.

The rest of us mounted up and headed for the house in Ontario. It was only a 15 minute drive. We had not gone back home after renting the equipment but found a parking lot and sat around waiting for the call.

Irvin and Sam had rigged the camera with two bands to hold it in place. All Irvin would need to do was to run the straps around the pole and twist the bands tight to hold it in place. We had no way to remote the signal from the camera to the computer at home, which meant that someone would still have to be in the area around the clock. The transmitter in the camera had a short range, something like one mile, Irvin said. We could park at the nearest strip mall and monitor the picture from a portable computer.

All of us went to the nearest mall, which was only about a quarter of a mile away and tried out the camera features. It had a zoom feature and could be moved left and right to a small degree.

"If someone shows up at the house, use the zoom to try to get a clear picture of the visitors. Save all those to a separate file," I cautioned.

"Do we still follow him if he leaves?" Matt asked.

"By all means. He could possibly lead us to others and we want to document every one he has contact with. It might be a good idea to keep a journal of his activities. Knowing his habits might come in handy at some point," I replied.

We left Matt and Larry in place and returned to our house. I didn't see much more we could do so we all hit the sack early.

I drove to Westlake the next day and briefed Bill Hardwick on what we had learned.

I told him about Ellen Norton's contact with Carolyn and that we had gotten an identity of the Saudi Carolyn had met in Cannes. I didn't tell him about the time in Saudi Arabia because it wasn't pertinent to the case and the CIA might frown on my letting the cat out of the bag.

I finished with the explanation that we had gone through Carolyn's belongings again and found a card with a license number on it. "We ran the plates and got an ID on the car. I think that Carolyn recognized that she was being followed and wrote the license number down. We found it at the bottom of a bedside stand when the drawers were pulled out. I don't know if she did that purposely or if it just got displaced in the move," I said.

"What are you doing about the suspect now?" Bill asked.

"Following him 24/7. I don't believe he abducted Carolyn alone and with luck one of his companions might show up."

I thought of telling him about the camera but decided against it.

"It's looking more and more like a homicide, don't you think?" Bill asked.

"I think that is pretty definite. The problem now is to find out what they did with the body. There's not enough evidence to even arrest them if we can't come up with a corpse. Nobody saw them and five years after the fact there will certainly not be forensic evidence. And I don't believe this guy would cop a plea," I said.

"You're probably right. I wish you luck," he said.

I was alone this time and just after I left Westlake my phone rang. It was Weatherly.

"Just wanted to let you know that the two suspects in the Middle East delivered five black men to the airport in Riyadh not long ago. The five boarded planes destined to Mexico City. I think they will try to infiltrate the bombers across the Mexican border. The other two will probably not move until they get the word that the goats have arrived safely. What's happening on your end?"

"We got an identity on the car that was following Carolyn just before she went missing and ran the number to get an ID on the owner. He is Arabic. Name is Usha Bin Dahari. I am having him watched around the clock. If he is the contact as I suspect, then he will have to coordinate with someone to get the troops across the border."

"Don't do anything to spook him. He is the link that will let us know what they are really planning," he said.

"I am going to have one of my guys bug his house if we can find a good opportunity. I have a video camera monitoring the entrance to his house. It is well placed and should not be discovered. I will send you pictures of all his visitors. So far he hasn't had any, but we have only been on him two days."

"You might want to touch base with Homeland Security. I imagine they will be interested in what you just told me."

"I hadn't thought about that but it is a good point. I will call the Director and see what she wants to do," I said.

When I got back to the house I called the number Ansel Devlin gave me. He answered right away.

I identified myself and said, "I have a line on a possible terrorist. He also happens to be the person who was following the missing woman five years ago. We have him under surveillance and will get photos of any contacts he has. I informed the CIA and they suggested that you folks would have an interest in this."

"He was right about that. Can you make another quick trip to Washington?"

"As long as you are paying for it," I answered.

He laughed. "Fly commercial and let me know if you will be at Dulles or National. I will have someone meet you and bring you here. I know the Director will be interested to get your firsthand account of what went on across the pond. She got a brief from CIA but they don't always tell you everything if you take my meaning."

"I will take a late flight and try to get there in the early morning hours. I will call with the travel arrangements."

I called the airlines and arranged a flight that left at midnight. With the time change that would put me there in the morning hours. I then called Ansel and gave him the information.

Chapter 16

Sam took me to the airport and dropped me off. I checked in and went to the security checkpoint. I had left my pistol at home, but my badge had enough metal to set the alarm off.

Once on the airplane I zonked out and slept most of the way across the country.

I hadn't brought any luggage and when I got off the plane and entered the terminal area I saw a man holding a sign up with Kinkaid lettered on it.

I walked to the man and identified myself.

"My name is Barry and I am to take you to Nebraska Avenue," he said.

He led the way outside to a no parking zone where another man waited by the SUV. It was still early enough that we caught the last of the rush hour traffic. The ride to Nebraska Avenue took almost 40 minutes.

The man who met me in the terminal made a call, probably to Ansel, because when we got to the entrance to the building he was waiting for me.

He walked me around the security apparatus and we headed for the Director's office.

Ansel grabbed some coffee for us on the way in.

I was greeted cordially and we got down to business.

"Okay, what happened in Saudi Arabia?" the Director asked.

"I and three of my people flew over using our own passports. Weatherly provided all the funding and materials we needed. Sam, the big guy who was with me last time, got a job in Sarraf's oil field. The rest of us kept an eye on Sarraf. He eventually led us to another man, who led us to two more near a mosque. We got pictures and forwarded them to the Brits and CIA. Two of the three at the mosque the CIA definitely identified as terrorists. In my mind that definitely linked Sarraf to terrorists and that was our objective. I still wanted to get an identity of the killers in L.A. but didn't see that as likely unless we could get a bug planted, which was almost impossible without being conversant in the language."

"I had about decided that we would give it one more day and then come back home. Sam called late in the day and asked us to meet him near the barracks where they housed the oil field workers. One of his co-workers had an accident and Sam had helped him out. There were six Somali's marking time at the oil field until time for their mission. The guy who got hurt was standing near a lift loaded with oil piping when the load suddenly fell all around him. The others paid no attention but Sam helped him out and splinted his leg, which was broken, and got him back to the barracks. That night when the work crew returned, no one paid any attention to him, even to say, 'boy you were lucky', or 'how you feeling man'."

"Sam pointed this out to the young man and intimated that the supposed accident was intentional. The young man thought it over and decided that Sam was right. He told him the story about how he and five others had been recruited in Somalia for a holy mission. The only prerequisite was that those chosen must speak passable English. He didn't care what the mission was. At least it would get him out of Somalia."

"Hakim told Sam all he knew, which turned out to be more than we had bargained for. The six were to do great damage somewhere in the U.S. The target area had been identified as Los Angeles. Hakim told his recruiter that was fine with him, because he really wanted to visit Disneyland. The recruiter had a startled look according to Hakim, making him think that Disneyland might be the target."

"I called Weatherly and asked him to arrange to get us out of there, which he did. We flew to Iraq in a spook helicopter then to Germany, and finally to McGuire AFB. We ended up in a CIA safe house where they interrogated the poor kid for hours."

"While we were there I had an encounter with Carolyn's spirit, or ghost if you prefer. It was very quick and she only said a name and disappeared. The name was Usha Bin Dahari. He's the guy we are watching in L.A., actually Ontario. What has the CIA told you?" I asked.

"Not much. They said they had identified a couple of terrorists and gave us pictures for our watch list. They made no mention that the target area was L.A. I suspect that they want to nab the culprits someplace after they take off from Saudi Arabia. They could be coordinating with the British, since the flight will probably stop in London."

"I am pretty sure the Brits are going to make Sarraf disappear at the first opportunity. Weatherly told me that the five remaining bombers had boarded a plane for Mexico City. I suspect they will try to infiltrate them across the border between San Diego and the Arizona border. To do that our boy Usha Bin Dahari will have to coordinate their pickup. I don't see him doing that himself. He will probably hire Mexicans from Los Angeles who are into smuggling people across the border. If he meets with anyone we should know about it, especially if he brings them home with him."

"What kind of neighborhood does he live in?"

"Lower middle class. The houses are on sizable individual lots and about half of the residents keep their yards in respectable shape. Others just let the weeds grow. It's one of those areas where the well-off ran into misfortune and had to move down, and those in the lower status had some luck and moved up. We mounted a camera facing his house on a utility pole. We have to be within range of the signal to get the feed, but we do that from a strip mall parking lot. When he leaves we check the direction and try to pick him up and follow."

"You think that the people in Saudi Arabia will wait to get word that the sacrificial lambs have arrived before they attempt to enter the country?" she asked.

"That would be the way I would do it. If they don't have good papers they may very well try the ploy they are using to get the others here," I said.

"What would you say to a few of our people joining forces with you to do the surveillance?" Ansel asked.

"I don't have a problem with it. We don't have any arrest authority and they would provide that if it becomes necessary. The main thing I want is to locate the body of Carolyn Clayton so the family will have some closure. I also want to see them punished, but we can take care of that little detail if they resist arrest," I said. "I believe Dahari was working with at least one, possibly two others when they abducted her. It's possible that they can't even lead me to the place where they disposed of the body."

"I will send half a dozen agents to give you a hand. I will also make it clear that they are on your turf and to pay attention to what you say," the Director said.

"I can pair them up with my people who are doing the job now but when I plant the bugs in Dahari's house, if we have the opportunity, I don't want any resistance because of the legal aspects. The tapes would not be legal in court but I am more concerned with learning for sure where the target is and finding ties to other terrorists," I said.

"I will make it clear to those selected that you are in charge," Ansel said.

We decided on the best way to join our forces up. I told Ansel to just have them call me when they were in the area and I would give them directions to the house. Since I didn't have an office that was the best I could do.

I was on a plane back to L.A. before the end of the day.

Chapter 17

When I got back to L.A. I called Sam and asked him to pick me up.

We got back to the house and I briefed everyone, with the exception of Matt, who had the watch on Dahari.

"I don't think there is much love lost between DHS and CIA. Weatherly didn't give them the full story. For example he didn't even mention Hakim and what he provided and apparently he didn't tell them about the group flying to Mexico City. I can understand why he didn't mention those going to Mexico City. He had just told me and probably thought I would pass along that little tidbit, but it doesn't make a lot of sense to me that they wouldn't mention Hakim, since he was the source of most of the information."

"Turf wars. The CIA wants the credit if they manage to capture these guys, even though they don't have any authority to operate in the U.S. Bureaucratic in-fighting has been going on since the government was established. I simply want to make sure we don't lose track of Dahari." I continued.

Sam, Irvin and I had divided the phone messages and called them back. Irvin thought he had one case that might be worthwhile and Sam had a couple more. One was a 14 year old runaway who had been gone for almost a week. Another was about the computer in an automobile. Irvin thought that the automobile thing was simply a matter of providing about an hours' worth of instruction.

I asked James to call and set up an appointment with the people about the missing teen and take Matt with him. "Might as well cut your teeth on something from the ground up," I said.

The next morning I got a call from one of the HS agents. He had two other people with him and I gave him directions to the house.

It was almost time to change the surveillance shift and Sam was up next.

"Take my car and relieve Larry. Brief the guy who is going with you and try not to leave anything out," I said.

Irvin had gone to check on the automobile computer, and James and Matt had gone to see the guy with the missing teenager, so we had the house to ourselves. I offered beer or cokes and they declined both.

"How much do you know about the case?" I asked.

"Nothing really. We were told to pack our bags and come here and that you would brief us," the older of the two said.

"Okay, this all started when my detective firm took on a five year old case of a missing person. The young lady in question had a short affair in Cannes, France just after graduating from college. She snapped a picture of him with another man in a restaurant. He didn't know she had taken the picture and they parted ways the next day."

"Leaving out all the small details, the picture turned out to be of Mohammad Sedique Khan, one of the London subway bombers. Of course he didn't survive the attack, but the picture linked our man to the terrorist. When a friend she was showing the pictures recognized the bomber she didn't know what to do. She had spent a week with the guy and thought it was coincidence that he was with the man. Here I am guessing, but she probably let him know that she had the picture and demanded an explanation. Shortly thereafter she went missing. The police had no clues and the case just sat on the shelf."

"Her parents called me and asked if I would look into the matter. Since they could afford my fees I told them I would do some preliminary work and see what it looked like before agreeing to go all out."

I skimmed over the rest of it until I got to the part about Saudi Arabia. "We knew the identity of Sarraf, the man our client's daughter had met in Cannes and watched his house for almost two weeks in the outskirts of Riyadh. Sam, the big guy who just left, got a job in the oil field of the suspect. There he found evidence of a plot to commit a terrorist attack in the U.S. We think it is going to take place at Disneyland. The remaining five bombers are by now in Mexico preparing to cross the border. Two others are waiting in Saudi Arabia to get word that the five have made it safely. The guy we are watching is the contact in the local area, and I suspect is the guy who killed my client's daughter. We have a camera mounted on a utility pole across the street from his house so we monitor all of his activity. If he leaves the house we try to pick him up and follow. That's it in a nutshell."

"So this guy you are watching has ties to terrorists," one of them said.

"We haven't had him in the presence of any known terrorists, but the missing girl had his license plate number written on the back of one of her business cards. We only recently found that. I have no doubt that he is involved because the ghost of the missing girl told me his name," I said.

"Maybe you had better back up and say that again."

"Carolyn Clayton's ghost gave me his name."

"Are we supposed to believe this or are you having a bit of fun?"

"I don't care if you believe it or not but the information is factual."

Doug, the older of the two, said, "Does the Director know about this?"

"Of course. Why do you think you are here?"

"I mean about the ghost part."

"The answer to that is yes. She doesn't care where the information comes from as long as it is valid, and I could take about an hour and run you through all the little things and you would be convinced as well."

"So what do we do now? It was made very clear to us that you are calling the shots," Doug said.

"I want to team you guys up with one of mine. They know the layout and the area. If we have an opportunity I want to place a listening device in the suspect's house. My contact at CIA will let me know if any of the group makes it into the country. They flew to Mexico City yesterday. I believe they will try to cross the border illegally. The CIA probably has them under surveillance, and your Director knows the circumstances and has already alerted the border patrol to increase their vigilance. As to the two in Saudi Arabia, it is possible that they will try to enter the country under their own names. Both are on the terrorist watch list and it is just possible that they will either use aliases or try to enter through Mexico or Canada."

"You are hoping that the guy we will be watching will lead to others?"

"Yes. I don't believe he could have carried out the abduction of my client's daughter without help. Of course that took place more than five years ago and the situation might not be the same. Still, he had ties to Sarraf then and I don't believe that will have changed," I said.

"Tell me more about this ghost thing," Doug said.

"Are you familiar with the heroin and human smuggling cases that were on the news a few weeks ago?"

"Yes. It was a high profile bust."

"Well that started out as a search for the killers of two people who died several years earlier. The husband of the woman came to me and told me he had visions of his wife telling him that she and their son had been murdered. That was very strange because the coroner had ruled the deaths natural. I told him I would look into the matter and encountered a psychic who told me the same thing. I was skeptical, but when two people, hundreds of miles from each other had the same experiences it gave me pause to reflect on the reality of what I was being told."

"During my efforts to find out if the wife and son had actually been murdered there were additional appearances of the woman's ghost. I uncovered enough to convince me that the wife and son had indeed been murdered. I asked the client to have the bodies exhumed and he did so. Upon additional examination it was found that both had been poisoned. The woman even appeared to me as things were starting to get really hairy."

"The mafia was involved and 12 of them tried to kill me and my people in this very house. The point I am trying to make is that none of that would have been possible without the appearances of the ghost."

"I remember you now. You did an interview with the news people after they tried to kill you here," he said.

"Yes but the point I was trying to make is that there are in fact ghosts or spirits who can and do appear to certain people. I have no idea about the mechanics of the phenomenon but I do know that it happens. Carolyn's ghost appeared to the psychic I work with and gave her a name that led to unraveling the events leading up to the disappearance of Carolyn Clayton. Then when I was in Saudi Arabia she appeared to me and gave me the name of the man we are now watching. I might add that the psychic has a doctorate in applied psychology, so she is not some fake swami."

"What are you getting out of this?"

"I am being paid by my client to find out what really happened to his daughter, but through our investigation into the matter we linked the money man behind the London attack in 2005 to one of the bombers. That led to a reward from the British government of £100,000."

"Then the CIA hired us to go to Saudi Arabia and get what we could on the guy we had identified as the money man. While there we uncovered a plot to mount a terrorist attack in the U.S. We even discovered where we believe it will take place."

"How often do these ghosts appear?"

"I have no idea. It isn't as if one could summon them. They operate on their own timetable. When the psychic had the first appearance of my client's daughter she gave me a name. It happened to be the name of a person we were investigating on another case. I thought that the message was that she was the guilty one in the other case. Lillian, the psychic, told me that she had never gotten a message from a ghost that didn't relate to the specific matter at hand. As it turned out the name was related to this case and was a key element in convincing me that Sarraf, the guy she met in Cannes, had been responsible for her death."

"You do know that planting a bug in someone's house is illegal?"

"Let him file a complaint if he finds it. I can then blame it on the CIA, since the bugs came from their stock."

"The CIA provided you with listening devices?"

"Yes in Saudi Arabia. We didn't have a chance to use them there and figured they might come in handy later, so we kept them. They also paid us very well for our time and efforts from their black funds."

"Then they don't know that you plan to use them here?"

"No, but it would make little difference. You can go to any electronics store and get the same thing for a couple of hundred dollars. We just had them on hand and figured why buy new ones when we already had what we needed."

"So you're actually getting paid by three sources?"

"Yes, but I don't bill the time we were in Saudi Arabia to my client. That would be unethical. The other things were just by products of the investigation."

"How long have you been in the investigative business?"

"This is only my second case. The first one was the human smuggling ring that made the news."

As we were talking my phone rang. It was Sam. "He just left the house. Do you want me to try to plant the bug?"

"Do you think you can enter the house without leaving any evidence of your entry?"

"I can try. If he didn't set the deadbolt I might be able to get in with my knife," he said.

"Give it a try but don't do anything that might put him onto the fact that he is under surveillance."

I hung the phone up. "That was Sam. Dahari just left the house. He is going to try to get inside to plant the bug."

"My guy with him might come in handy there. He has some experience with locks," Doug said.

Sam called back a bit later. "I got one in the living room and one in the kitchen. Is Irvin back yet?"

"No, what do you need?"

"We need the receiver for the bugs."

"That can wait until he gets back. Good job."

"Well, the bugs are in place."

"How many people do you have working for you?"

"There's Sam, who you have met, then there's Irvin, who is our computer guy, James who is sort of an analyst, and Larry and Matt, who do the grunt work. Plus of course, Lillian, our psychic. All the others are black, except for Lillian and myself."

"Do you find that a positive or a negative?

"I don't believe it makes any difference either way. They are all competent and can perform the tasks we encounter. If someone has a problem I would simply refuse to take the case. I think most people tend to make too much of a person's ethnicity. After we wrapped up the last case they all wanted to try to make a go of it so that's how the group came into being. All these guys are really intelligent. Sam and Irvin both have college degrees. James has spent time in Iraq, and Matt and Larry are young but eager. We all get along and there's no jealousy or resentment in the group. Once I accept a case and explain what we hope to achieve everyone pitches in and helps in whatever way they can. Just before we left for Saudi Arabia, James spent the night in the attic space of a convenience store to catch a thief in the act. We gave the information to the police and they arrested the clerk and his accomplice. James didn't complain about cramped and dirty conditions. He just looked at it as something that needed to be done. When Sam was required to work in the oil field in Saudi Arabia he was the same way. It was just something that went along with our mission."

"In many cases where a variety of people are thrown together that is a lot of bickering and discontent," Doug said.

"I think you will find those attitudes more prevalent in cases where the wages are poor and working conditions are not the best. On our last case, the client gave all of my people a bonus of $5,000 each. Sure they had risked their lives, and a couple even got shot, but they see the positive effects we have and appreciate that."

At that point Irvin came in. I introduced him to Doug and W.D. I then said, "Sam got a couple of bugs placed in Dahari's house. You will need to show the rest of us how the receiver operates."

"Why do I always get old people for clients?" he asked.

I laughed. "Probably because the younger potential clients are as knowledgeable as you are about computers. What was this one about?"

"He didn't know how to operate the computer in his car, which was one of the big Mercedes. I took the instruction book that came with the car and spent half an hour with him on that. We then moved to the car and I demonstrated the functions. It took a couple of hours and I was only going to charge him $200. He gave me $500. Since he could afford it I didn't offer to give it back."

"Said like a true capitalist," I said.

"When is Sam due to be relieved?"

"Not for a couple of hours."

I got another phone call and it was the other three HS people. I gave them directions to the house.

When they arrived it turned out that two of them were black.

As the introductions were being made one of the blacks from HS made the comment that it was nice to see other blacks involved in the case.

Irvin looked all around in an obvious manner. "I don't see any other blacks here. We're all color blind. We aren't black or white, or yellow, we're just people doing a job."

The one who made the comment said, "I didn't mean that the way it sounded. I just meant that it was unusual to have a black as part of an investigative firm."

"Well you are truly in for a surprise. The only non-black face in the firm is Brad, and he owns the company," Irvin said.

"Don't forget Lillian," I said.

"Oh, that's right, sorry, make that two. And for your edification, of the five blacks in the firm, three of us have college degrees and the other two are a lot smarter than the average man on the street. We work together because we respect each other and because we are doing work that pays well and is very satisfying in other ways. There's no racial animosity here and I would appreciate it if you don't try to sow the seeds."

"I give up," the other said. "I didn't mean to get your hackles up. I was just saying that you don't normally find blacks in the position you're in."

"Forget it. I just get defensive when someone doesn't understand that it is not the color of the skin but the size of the brain that really makes the difference."

"With that out of the way, you gents can have beer, soda, or whatever else is in the refrigerator. I will then brief you about what is going on. I have already briefed these two, I said, indicating Doug and W.D.

I started this brief with the question, "Do you believe in ghosts."

Both the blacks raised their hands.

I went through the entire case from the start again. When I was finished the white agent said, "You really believe in that crap?"

"Yes, I do, but only because they have appeared to me, and in every case provided information that dealt with the case I was working on."

"The plan is to join each of you up with one of my people for the stake-out. Sam just today got the bugs placed. Irvin is going to give us a quick tutorial on how to operate the receiver. Both the camera feed and the audio, if there is any, will be monitored by the stake-out crew. We aren't looking for legal evidence, but are trying to learn the suspect's contacts. Since the five Somali's are in Mexico he will have to be contacted soon to get instructions about how to meet them. I'm thinking we need two teams per shift so that we can follow him when he leaves the house. So far that part of the surveillance has been very loose. If we could pick him up we followed, if not then we just went back to the parking lot to wait for his return."

"It doesn't bother you that planting bugs in a private residence without a court order is illegal?" the white agent asked.

"Nope. This guy is connected to a murder case, and is in the process of committing a terrorist act against the U.S. If he finds the bug he can report it to the police, but somehow I don't see that as a viable option for him. My philosophy is to fight fire with fire."

"If he should discover them and report it HS would be in trouble."

"Not to worry. If it comes to that I will take the heat and keep your organization out of it."

Matt and Larry made an appearance and introductions were made.

Chapter 18

I called Sam and told him to break off the surveillance just after 7:00 p.m. I wanted everyone present to explain the procedures we would use to follow Dahari.

Irvin gave us a short lecture on the receiver. It wasn't very complicated but I wanted everyone to know how to save conversations that were connected to what we were doing. "I am particularly interested in any conversations related to bomb making. Someone in the local area is going to have to provide the explosives and we need a line on him."

"How do you know the suspects in Mexico won't make their own?"

"Because the one we have said that the recruiter stated that the only skill necessary for the mission was a pretty good grasp of the English language," I said.

"You mean you captured one?"

"Tell them the story Sam."

Sam told about how he had gotten a job in the oil field of our suspect in Saudi Arabia and how the pipes had fallen on Hakim. Then after the others totally ignored him that night how Hakim had told him what was planned. He then told how we had all gotten out of Saudi Arabia.

"We know nothing about that," Doug said.

"Your Director didn't either when I briefed her three days ago. He is in the hands of the CIA and is being kept under wraps until this situation is resolved. He will then be given a work permit and we will find a job for him," I said.

"You mean you personally will find a job for him?" another asked.

"I already have one lined up," I said.

"Being from Somalia I assume this guy is black," another added.

"Blacker than even Sam, but he is very intelligent and only got involved in this thing as a way to get out of Somalia. He had no idea that it was a suicide mission. On top of that he only paid lip service to the Islamic faith out of self-defense. If all else fails I will use him in some capacity with the firm," I said.

"How would you use him?"

"I haven't the foggiest idea, but he is very observant and perceptive. When he mentioned that he would like to go to Disneyland he read the expression of the recruiter to mean that Disneyland is the target. I would put my money of his assessment."

"Back to the business at hand. I think we need two cars with two men each. One will stay in the parking lot to monitor the feeds. The other car will find someplace in the opposite direction so they can pick Dahari up when he leaves the house. If he meets anyone I want pictures of those he contacts. Make sure there are cameras in both cars. We have a good quality one, and if you new guys don't have one we will go buy one. It is imperative that we get pictures of everyone he meets."

The teams were chosen and a schedule set up. "We will use the house here as the command post. All meetings and such will be held here."

The surveillance picked up again the following morning. It appeared that the bugs worked as advertised and we settled into a routine right away.

Dahari didn't go out often, and when he did his movements were closely monitored.

One phone call we recorded might have been from one of his fellow conspirators. Although we only got his side of the conversation we all thought the call was related. His side went something like this:

"Hello."

"No I haven't heard anything yet."

"Have you got all the materials?"

"Well you had better get everything ready. I expect to get a call anytime now."

"They wired $5,000 to my account last week. If you are short of funds I will give you what you need."

"Probably the day after tomorrow."

"I will see you then."

John Buckner

The recording was nothing to write home about, but the mention of the money, coupled with the comment that he had not heard anything yet, led me to believe that he had not heard from Sarraf's people about the infiltration of the five Somali's. It wasn't much, but it was progress.

"I think the reference to the day after tomorrow might have been a meeting between Dahari and the caller," Irvin said.

"It also could have been the tentative arrival of the group from Mexico City," I added.

"Either way we can look for some action in two days' time," Sam said.

I called Weatherly and asked, "what's the story on our boys to the south?'

"Still making their way toward you. I will call when they get close. What is happening on your end?"

"We have an individual under surveillance. I now have half a dozen DHS guys helping out. We have both audio and visual coverage so he can't do much without our knowing about it."

"Your package is in the mail. I will be in touch."

I told the others that the ones in Mexico weren't near the border yet and that Weatherly would call when they got close.

The next day I called both the Clayton's and Lillian. I briefed the Clayton's in the morning and had lunch with Lillian and Merle.

I told the Clayton's, "We have surveillance set up on the guy who matched the license plate number we found in Carolyn's belongings. It appears that he was the one who set up her abduction. I am hoping that he leads us to his accomplices. Right now we are waiting to find out who is making the bombs the terrorists plan to use."

"You don't think Carolyn might still be alive?" Mrs. Clayton asked.

"I believe it is a foregone conclusion that she is dead. Her spirit would not have appeared to Lillian and me if she was still alive. I hope to determine what happened once we identify the others in the area tied to Dahari. It won't be in a court of law, but once we identify those involved they will be punished," I said.

161

"Don't you go doing anything that will get you into trouble," she said.

"I won't. If they don't resist then they will be tried as terrorists and get a pretty stiff prison sentence. My preference would be that they resist arrest, but either way they will pay," I said.

"Have you heard any more about the boy you brought back with you?" Harry asked.

"I talked to Weatherly last night. They still have him in a safe house. He and Sam just might be the only ones who can positively identify the five coming in from Mexico. I hadn't thought of that until just this moment."

When I got to Lillian's house she had prepared a light lunch and we sat around the table talking about the case.

"You know, I was quite surprised when you told me that Carolyn had been in contact with you. It seems you are a good conduit to the spirit world. That's twice now, or is it three times," she said with a chuckle.

"My heart is pure and my intentions honorable. What more could you ask for," I replied.

"You say that jokingly, but I believe those are exactly the prerequisites the spirits look for in those they contact."

"How would they know those things?"

"I have no idea. Since she contacted you while you were half way around the world I suspect that time and space are of no significance in their world. I guess I will have to wait until I die to see how it all works."

"Well, let's hope it isn't soon," I said.

Merle added an "amen" to that.

Nothing of significance happened the next couple of days, unless you want to consider the delivery of $80,000 in a plain cardboard box. When it came I signed for it and put it in my bedroom closet. I wanted all the guys together when I opened it.

The opportunity didn't present itself until late that night.

I called them together and said, "I have a surprise for you." I then opened the box. It contained 16 stacks of 100 dollar bills banded in $5,000 packets. Only two of the HS guys were there and they were mystified by the large amount of money.

"This is our payday from Saudi Arabia. We are going to split it equally among all of us. Just don't go trying to deposit all of it into the same bank account or the IRS will be on you like flies on horse droppings. The money will never appear on any official documents so keep it low key."

"The money from the British will go into our operating fund. We might run on hard times when we don't make enough to meet our payroll and that will be insurance against those times."

"Where did the money come from?" the HS agent asked.

"From the CIA's black budget. That was our payment for the time we spent over there. The way it was explained to me, they pay informants more than that and we certainly earned the money as far as results go."

"Maybe I should change jobs and come to work for you," he said.

"This was just a bountiful harvest. There will be a lot of small cases before we happen upon something like this again," I said.

"We do make a decent living though," Sam offered.

We all had a beer to celebrate.

The next day was the day we thought Dahari would meet one of his cohorts. We had three cars with two people each near his house and when he left just before 11:00 a.m. we all followed. I didn't want to lose him and kept a closer tail, alternating cars as the one nearest him. He drove for about 15 minutes and turned off the main thoroughfare onto a less travelled road. We dropped back a bit but still kept him in sight. He eventually turned into a housing tract and the car nearest him kept going. The two behind made the same turn.

I was in the car that had been closest and I had driven on past. I found a place to turn around and headed back to the turnoff the others had taken. My phone rang and I used the blue tooth to answer it.

"He turned on Elm Street," James said. "Sam is on him. I kept going and will double back."

"Roger, Elm Street," I replied and killed the connection.

Elm Street was about six streets into the development and I didn't know which way to turn when I got there. I pulled to the curb and speed dialed James' number.

"Which way," I asked when he answered.

"Right. Sorry man."

I made the turn and my phone rang again.

It was Sam. "He turned into the driveway of 4355 to the left. I went on past and am now turning around."

I drove slowly, looking for house numbers to get a feel for how far away I might be. I found I was already in the 4100's and looked for a likely place to park. I noticed a for sale sign on a house and pulled into the driveway.

I went to the porch and rang the bell. I waited for a good minute and rang the bell again. When no one answered I motioned for the HS guy with me to grab the camera and come on.

We walked down the street on the right side until we came to 4355. Dahari's car was in the driveway but no one was in sight.

We strolled on by and met Sam and his HS buddy coming toward us.

The neighborhood was similar to the one in which Dahari lived. Some of the yards were kept up and some were not. Sam and his partner were on the other side of the street and I waved in a neighborly fashion. I then took out my phone and called Sam.

"I parked about half a block down in the driveway of a house for sale. It is too far to get a picture so we are going to have to do the strolling bit until something happens. James should be ahead of you. Fill him in when you meet him."

Just then the light came on in the garage of the house Dahari was visiting. The door did not open but the light spilled through the paper covering the glass panels of the garage. It had apparently been put there for the purpose of keeping others from seeing inside.

I told the man with me, "I will give you odds that we are looking at the place where the bombs are being assembled."

"I wouldn't bet against you on that," he replied.

We spent the better part of two hours walking up and down the street, keeping enough separation so that when one group got out of sight of the house another picked it up from the opposite direction.

When Dahari came out the front door the man who apparently lived there stood in the doorway finishing their conversation. Dahari had his back to us but the other party was framed in the door way. I took a quick picture, then took another when he turned his head away from us.

He came on out of the house and walked with Dahari toward the car. I got another picture.

When Dahari left I called James and told him to follow, just in case he was meeting someone else that day. Sam and I and our HS partners stayed in the area. I wanted to get a look at the back yard of the house, and if possible, a glimpse through a window into the garage.

It was only a short while later that the owner of the house left as well. I quickly called Sam and told him to follow this one. After he was well away from the area I went to the porch and rang the bell. I waited and rang again. When there was still no response I told my partner that we were going to have a look.

The lot had a six foot redwood fence surrounding the back yard. There was a walkthrough gate and it was not locked. The two of us went into the back yard. The side door from the garage was inside the fenced area and we tried the door. It would be stupid to leave the door unlocked, but stranger things had happened and I didn't want to pass up the opportunity.

The door was, of course, locked, but we were rewarded with the aroma of fertilizer coming from the garage. Fertilizer is one of the elements used to construct bombs. The back yard was a tangle of grass and weeds. It didn't appear to have had any TLC for at least six weeks.

We made our way back to the car and headed back to the house. I figured James or Sam would call when they had something to report. I was also anxious to find out if the pictures were any good.

Irvin downloaded the pictures and they were pretty good. The first showed the man at a bit of an angle, but his features could be seen easily. The second was in semi profile and showed the right side of his face. Irvin blew the picture up and we could see a white scar from his ear almost to his collarbone. This one would be easy to identify later.

Sam and his partner came in shortly thereafter and he said, "The dude went to the Lowe's garden center and purchased a shit-load of fertilizer. He had trouble getting it all into his car."

"Well he certainly doesn't plan to use it on his lawn. The back yard doesn't look as if has been touched in six weeks or more," I said.

"If we try to add him to our surveillance package we are going to be stretched pretty thin. I am going to call the Director and ask for more people."

"That makes sense. With what's going on now and the prospect of the five in Mexico entering the picture we will really be thin."

"I will call first thing in the morning, although Ansel will probably answer his phone. Let me give it a try."

I dialed the number and he answered on the second ring.

"Calling a bit late aren't you," he said by way of greeting.

"We have identified another player and need additional people to do surveillance," I said.

"Are you sure this guy is a player?"

"Our boy visited him at home and he went to Lowe's and purchased a trunk load of fertilizer. His yard could certainly use it, but the back hasn't been touched by any garden implement in quite a while. Also, we detected a strong smell of fertilizer from his garage while he was away from the house. I think this guy is the bomb maker," I said.

"How many more do you want?"

"I think at least half a dozen more. If I am correct there's at least one more player in the area that we don't know about yet."

"I will have to clear it with the Director in the morning but I don't think there will be any opposition. I will call you after we have had time to have coffee in the morning," he said.

"Thanks Ansel. Sorry for waking you in the middle of the night."

"I will probably get a chance to return the favor before this is over."

The next time Dahari went out his destination was the mosque. When I found out where he was we all converged on the location with cameras at the ready. We snapped pictures of every male between 18 and 50 as they came out, though none of them had been seen with Dahari. When he did come out he was in the company to two other men about his age, and those we made sure to get on film. The three had a somewhat lengthy conversation in the parking lot and between three teams we got enough pictures to fill a scrapbook.

Six more DHS agents arrived the day after I talked to Ansel.

The house was getting a bit crowded with so many people in and out. I suggested that the latest crew work out of their hotel, or get some space from one of the local law enforcement agencies. They would take over surveillance of the guy who had bought the fertilizer.

The pictures we had taken I forwarded to Ansel. He was in a better position to have them evaluated than I was.

He called me later and said that they got a hit on one of the guys from the mosque, though they couldn't put a name to the face.

Dahari made a trip to East L.A. where he met with a man of Mexican extraction. We again got pictures. I surmised that he was probably making arrangements to transport the Somali's when they crossed the border.

I didn't know how we were going to deal with the problem when they arrived. To me it made sense to allow them to all get together and bust them all at the same time. Odds were that they would be housed with the guy who was making the bombs.

I knew, however, that the decision was not mine to make. I wanted to get a better line on the two from the mosque but we had not followed them when they left. I didn't have any way to run them down to a specific address.

We picked up more audio from Dahari. Whoever he was talking to was apparently giving directions for the attack.

His side of the conversation was:

"Hello."

"And it is good to hear from you."

"Yes, everything seems to be going fine. I am waiting to hear something from the people down south. I have already arranged for someone to meet them and bring them to me. They will stay with Mustapha until the time comes."

"I will need more money. I had to purchase additional materials for the project, and I had to pay the person who will meet the new arrivals $2,000."

"You have the bank routing numbers so just transfer it to the account."

"I am not sure at this point. Perhaps a week, perhaps a bit longer. A lot will depend on how cooperative the new arrivals are. Do they know the nature of the project?"

"I mean do they know that they will become martyrs?"

"I will need to come up with some plausible plan to keep them in the dark. I will let them think that they are to plant the packages and then exit the place. Mustapha can rig them to be detonated by remote control. It won't matter so much where they are. Anyplace inside will do a lot of damage."

"I don't know. Maybe we should have planned it so that they can escape."

"I will do as you order."

"And may Allah be with you as well."

After listening to the recording I called Ansel and played the tape for him.

"Looks like the time line is seven to ten days," he said.

"That's assuming we allow the Somali's to enter the country. What are your thoughts on that?" I asked.

"It would be better if we could round them all up at once. I want to make damn sure that the explosives don't leave the house where they are being made."

"Have the guys at the border been given any directions for dealing with them?"

"Yes, and I have additional people from our organization with them."

"Then I will keep plugging away here."

Chapter 19

We continued to monitor Dahari. On the second day after he had talked with the people in the mosque parking lot one of them showed up at his house. We got the license plate number and while he was still at the house the DHS guy ran the number. That resulted in a name and address not too far from where Dahari lived.

He spent almost an hour in the house with Dahari. The bug picked up all their conversation.

The visitor, whose name was Ali, wanted to know if the project was on schedule.

"We are almost ready. A lot will depend on how soon the group of Somali's arrive. They didn't tell them that it was a suicide mission and we have to keep that from them. Have you checked out the area where we want to get the packages over the fence?"

"I have looked at it twice. Once from the inside and again from the outside. The foliage inside the fence is pretty thick and unless someone comes out the back of one of the retail places it should work as we planned," Ali said.

"How will we get them to the park?"

"You, me and Mustapha can all drive and carry a couple in each car. The explosive packages will take up a good deal of room in Mustapha's trunk. We don't want the detonators in the same vehicle, so either you or I will transport those," Dahari said.

"This should be a great blow to the infidels," Ali said.

"Not as much fun as we had with the woman, but still very satisfying," Dahari said.

I assumed he was talking about Carolyn.

"It is strange that no one has found the body yet. That place was not very desolate," Ali said.

"It is possible that animals dragged the body away," Dahari said.

"I don't think they have animals large enough to do that," Ali said.

"It has been five years and the body will have decayed beyond recognition in any case."

"Did Mustapha have enough C-4 for the detonators to trigger?"

"Yes, he has had that for quite some time. I don't know where it came from, but it was delivered to him almost two months ago when the planning for the mission started," Dahari said.

"Choosing the amusement park was a stroke of genius. We will pick a day when they are very busy and the casualties should be in the hundreds," Ali said.

"I want to be close enough to witness the event. After we deliver the materials we will wait in the parking lot," Dahari said.

"If this works well we might try to mount an attack on the park over on the 5 freeway. It used to be called Magic Mountain. I don't know if it still has the same name or not."

"One thing at a time. I am worried that something might go wrong with the people trying to cross over from Mexico."

"Don't worry. Everything will be fine."

I suggested to the senior HS agent that he send a couple of people to the address we had gotten for Ali and see what the place looked like while he was still with Dahari.

He made the call and two men left immediately for the address.

"That last conversation proves that Dahari and Ali were in on the murder of Carolyn Clayton," I said.

"Yes, but it will not hold up in a court of law," W.D., the DHS agent with me, said.

"I don't plan to let it get to a court of law. You've heard the old saying that what's good for the goose is good for the gander, haven't you?"

"You can't just kill him. That would put you in the same category as him, not to mention that it is against the law."

"I think he can be provoked into taking some sort of action that would provide grounds for self-defense. That's essentially how we goaded the mafia goons into attacking the house here," I said.

"I don't want to hear about that," he said.

"I wasn't going to tell you anyway. I haven't quite got it all figured out myself yet," I said.

My phone rang and I glanced at the caller ID. It was a Washington area code, Weatherly's I thought.

"Hello," I said.

"Weatherly here," he said. "Your boys are getting close to the border. I think they will try to cross tomorrow or the next night."

"Has anyone given any thought to recognition? I believe Hakim is the only one who can make a positive ID."

"What are you suggesting?"

"That you send Hakim to us. I will take care of him until this is over."

"He really is just a kid and knew nothing about anything other than his recruitment. I will have one of my men escort him on the plane. I will give my man your number and have him pass on the flight information. How goes the surveillance?"

"We have at least three people involved at this end. All are under constant surveillance. One of them confirmed that they had been responsible for Carolyn's death. They also confirmed that Disneyland is the target. We know where the bombs are being assembled and have a four man team watching that location. They also confirmed that the Somali's do not know that it is supposed to be a suicide mission. They plan to get the Somali's into the park and pass the packages over the fence. Then before they have time to plant the packages they will remotely detonate the explosives. That way it will appear to be a suicide attack and no one will know the difference, except us of course."

"How far along are you going to allow them to get before busting them?"

"I don't know. That is up to DHS. I imagine they will wait at least until they join up with the people here. Better to try to get them all at once. Is Sarraf still among the living?"

"To the best of my knowledge. My people are still watching the men he met with at the mosque. I think they will try to get into the country once they are sure the Somali's made it. I will let you know when they are on the move."

To the DHS man I said, "Looks like things are coming together. The Somali's are near the border and Weatherly thinks they will try to cross either tomorrow night or the night after. Have you guys figured out how to handle this yet?"

"I was told to take my directions from you. What do you recommend?"

"I would allow the ones crossing the border to get this far. I believe Dahari will put them up with the guy making the bombs. That way you can catch the whole bunch in the act with the explosives as evidence. It would be nice if we could do that when Dahari was at the same location because we don't have any evidence linking him directly to the plot, other than his knowing two of the accomplices, and I don't think that will stand up in court."

"By doing it that way we will have most of those involved and the bombs as evidence. I like that idea better than making arrests piecemeal."

"I'm going to call your director this evening and give her an update. I will run my idea by her and get her approval. That way we don't end up with egg on our faces if things get out of hand."

"What do you mean, out of hand?"

"I mean if they resist and we end up in a gunfight in a residential neighborhood," I said.

I got everyone together, other than those on duty, and explained what was happening.

"Weatherly is sending Hakim to us. Nobody seemed to realize that he and Sam are the only two who will be able to recognize them. My idea is to allow the Somali's to enter the country and keep tabs on them all the way to L.A. I believe they will be put up with Mustapha. If that happens we just wait for the opportune time and take them all at once. Any comments?"

"What about Dahari?" Irvin asked.

"I hope he will make an appearance at Mustapha's place. If not we will deal with him as a separate issue. You remember what we did to the mafia boss?"

Irvin nodded. "You think that will work with him?"

"We have enough facts to convince him that we are all knowing. I don't know what Muslims believe about that kind of thing, but it will certainly unnerve him, maybe force him to take some sort of action without thinking it through. It is certainly worth a try. The key will be getting access to his house while he is away."

"What are you talking about?" one of the HS agents asked.

"We had a case where we knew the head of the local mafia was involved in a murder and dope smuggling operations. We found out some personal information about him and rigged a speaker system beneath his bed. Once he was asleep we convinced him that the ghosts of people he had killed were seeking revenge. We goaded him into attacking this house, where we were waiting for him. We even evacuated the neighbors for the night and when they attacked there would be no collateral damage."

"How many were there?"

"Twelve, plus the drivers of two cars."

"How many men did you have?"

"Just what you see here, plus a detective from the county Sherriff's office."

"You took on 12 armed men with this group?"

"If they had a really large force we would have asked for help, but with the advantage of cover we figured we could handle them, and that turned out to be the case. The detective provided bullet proof vests for us. One guy caught one in the vest but other than that we didn't suffer any damage."

"And you spooked him by imitating a ghost?"

"Yes. We had his house bugged and knew when he got home and when he went to bed. We had enough factual information to convince him that we were all knowing. Catholics believe in that sort of thing, so it didn't take much to convince him that the ghosts of his victims were out to get their revenge."

"I can't believe something like that worked."

"You have to remember we had been digging for six months and by that time we knew how the smuggling scheme worked, who the contact was in the company involved, and where the cargo was being loaded. We even found out his childhood nickname and used that."

"I still don't see how someone like that would be that gullible."

"If, in the middle of the night, someone spoke to you in your own bedroom when you couldn't see anyone and told you things about yourself that you thought no one knew I believe it would unnerve you pretty badly. In his case we had enough knowledge to hype him up pretty good. The clincher was when we told him that I was responsible for all his troubles. We also had the advantage of listening to the planning for the attack, so we knew when they were coming and how many of them there would be," I said."

"He couldn't tell where the voice was coming from?"

"We mounted speakers under his bed facing upward so the sound sort of came through the mattress. We tested the tactic before we set him up. Anyway it worked and that's all that matters."

I placed the call to the Director of DHS early enough to catch her in the office. When we made the connection I said, "It looks like we are getting close to some action. Weatherly called me and said the Somali's were near the border. What would you think about allowing them to get to L.A. so we can round up the entire bunch at once?"

"Are you sure they will be coming to L.A.?" she asked.

"I don't see any other alternative. You can have some of your people keep an eye on them from the time they enter the country. Hakim and Sam are the only ones who can positively identify them and Weatherly is sending Hakim to us. We know where the explosives are being assembled and believe that is where the Somali's will be quartered until time for the action."

"Do you have adequate forces to do what you want to do?"

"There are 12 of your people and six of mine. There will only be half a dozen of the bad guys, maybe seven or eight. We can seize the explosives at the same time and your case will be air tight," I said.

"What is the risk of collateral damage?"

"Pretty low I believe. I can't see the Somali's having any personal weapons. Dahari wouldn't be stupid enough to provide them guns until time for the attack, especially since they don't know that this is supposed to be a suicide mission."

"Let me speak to the senior agent."

I handed the phone to Doug.

He said, "Yes ma'am."

She apparently asked him what he thought about the plan because he replied, "I think it's the best way to round them all up at once. Brad's guys are as good as ours."

He next said, "Yes ma'am, I will do that."

He killed the phone and handed it back to me.

"She want's your group deputized so there will be no repercussions about using civilians for the raid."

"What does that entail?"

"Just issuing the oath to protect and defend, etc. etc."

Chapter 20

I got the call from the man escorting Hakim later that evening and Sam and I went to the airport to pick him up. His escort didn't even leave the airport, simply went to the ticket counter to arrange his flight back to Washington, I presume.

Hakim was glad to see us and had tears in his eyes as he hugged Sam.

We took him back to the house. I explained what was going on as we made our way back to the house.

The next evening I got a call from Weatherly telling me that tonight was the night according to his people who had been tracking the group in Mexico.

"I gave the coordinates for the crossing point to DHS. They should be able to pick them up easily once they enter the country."

Hakim seemed right at home with us. Irvin was even teaching him how to operate the computer. He came from a desolate village where no one had computers. He was enthralled with its operation.

Between the DHS people and mine we were keeping watch on Dahari, Mustapha and Ali. The bug in Dahari's house picked up the phone call telling him that his people were across the border and on the way to L.A.

"I will pick them up at 7:00 a.m. unless you call to tell me otherwise," he said toward the end of the call.

This was probably the coyote who picked them up at the border making the call.

We had Dahari under surveillance when he made the arrangements so we knew where he would be going. He could have made arrangements to pick them up elsewhere but that was not too likely. At any rate we would have three cars following him when he left his house.

The DHS agent had performed the obligatory oath and all my people were now provisional DHS agents.

All of us were up early the next morning. We left the house at 5:00 a.m. to be sure we were on time to follow Dahari when he left his house. It was about a 45 minute drive into L.A. where he had met the coyote, and with the morning traffic it was probably closer to an hour.

Dahari backed out of his driveway at 5:45 and the procession to L.A. got underway.

The three cars alternated staying close to him and he was none the wiser.

When he got to the destination he pulled into a steel building that had overhead doors. It looked like a warehouse from the outside.

Dahari was not inside more than 15 minutes when he pulled back out into traffic. The five Somali's were crammed into the car, three in the back and two in the front. It would not be a comfortable ride for them but probably better than the ride from the border, which typically saw as many as 15 to 20 Mexicans stuffed inside a panel truck or enclosed van.

We all followed the car back to Ontario, where, as I expected, he drove directly to Mustapha's house. He couldn't pull into the garage because it was filled with the explosive ingredients so they all got out and went to the front door. Mustapha met them at the door and motioned them inside.

It was chancy for three cars to be parked along the street where the house was located so we took turns driving by, about five minutes apart.

They were all inside for almost an hour. I would have given a lot to have heard the conversation but we had not had the foresight to bug Mustapha's house. He would probably be a bit more security conscious with the explosives in the garage.

When Dahari left one of the cars followed him home, then went to the parking lot to monitor the bug.

He apparently made a phone call because we didn't hear any chirps from his phone.

"The packages arrived safely," he said.

"How long before you join us?"

"I believe the best way is to fly to Canada, then make your way west. It is easy to cross the border. They don't have fences and probably very few guards. The Americans don't seem to be concerned that anyone would sneak across the border from Canada. If you leave today you can be in Canada tomorrow. You will then need to fly to the western part of the country. I would suggest either Vancouver or Banff. You can then rent a car and be to the border in a short time. Once you enter the U.S. you can take a bus or train to Los Angeles. It will take you three days at least."

He said, "Allah be with you," and ended the conversation.

I heard the tape that evening.

I asked the DHS agent, "What do you think? Want to wait until the other two arrive?"

"It would be better to get them all at once, but I don't feel comfortable that they will wait."

"We will be watching them 24/7, and if they attempt to leave we can be on them pretty quickly," I said.

I called the Director of DHS.

"Looks like the two from Saudi Arabia are on the way. Dahari suggested they enter through Canada. Canada probably has them on their watch list, so if you could convince them to allow the two to enter Canada it would be helpful. The plan is for them to fly west to either Vancouver or Banff. They will then come south and cross the border. From there either train or bus to L.A."

"Do you think it will be safe to wait that long?"

"We have them under constant surveillance. If they start to move early we will roll them up before they get underway. I believe they will wait for a weekend to carry out the attack so the park will be more crowded."

"Just be sure there are enough of our people nearby in case they are needed."

Mustapha and one of the Somali's left the house and were followed. They went to a grocery store and after half an hour came out with a cart loaded with food.

It takes a lot of food to feed six adults and I don't believe either Mustapha or Dahari had thought about that little item.

They went from the grocery store directly back to the house.

Ali hadn't been heard from for two days and I asked about him.

"He has been to the mosque a couple of times but otherwise stays at home," Doug said.

"I wonder what his involvement is."

"Probably to help get the explosive packages inside the park. That was all they talked about on the tape."

"It still strikes me as strange that he has not had any contact with the others since they arrived," I said.

"They might not want him to be seen by the Somali's. I don't know the reason that would be the case, but it is possible," Doug said.

"You know, it is strange that these guys don't seem to have jobs. All the time we have been following them none have done anything that looks like work," Doug said.

"Sarraf probably pays their expenses," I said.

"Even so you'd think that they would work someplace as a front for the terrorist stuff."

"The only thing that matters is that we know who they are and what they have planned," I said.

Weatherly called again late that night and told me that the two from Saudi Arabia had departed for London.

"They will probably take a flight from there to Ottawa. I didn't tell you but we got a conversation between them and Dahari. We only got his end of the conversation but he advised them to fly to Canada and enter the U.S. near Vancouver or Banff. The Director of DHS is talking to the Canadians to get them to allow them unfettered entry. They will probably have them followed if they cooperate. I don't believe the group here will take any action before they arrive. We have the five Somali's and three of the locals under constant surveillance. I imagine the time line is for this coming weekend. That gives the others two days to get here," I said.

We continued the surveillance on all the known players but nothing happened until Saturday morning. We got Dahari's end of a conversation that one of the Saudi Arabian's had initiated.

John Buckner

They were near Los Angeles but didn't know how to get to Dahari's house. He told them to make their way to Ontario and he would meet them at a Denny's restaurant.

"Do all your guys have bullet proof vests?" I asked Doug.

"Yeah. That's standard procedure."

"I am going to call a friend of mine and see if he will loan us enough for my guys. I don't expect a lot of gunplay, but better safe than sorry."

I called Eddie and asked him if we could borrow the vests again.

"What are you into now?"

"Bring the vests to my house and I will tell you all about it," I said.

He showed up just over an hour later with the vests.

I told him what was going down.

"You sure manage to stir up trouble everywhere you go," he said with a laugh.

"You want in on this?"

"How many of them are there?"

"Five Somali's, three from the area and two that are supposed to arrive any minute from Saudi Arabia."

"And how many do you have to oppose them?"

"Eighteen from HS plus my guys," I said.

"You're going to try to bottle them all up at the same time?" he asked.

"If we can. We have constant surveillance on all of them. I really hope we don't have to get into a battle. There are some questions about a five year old murder that need to be answered."

"Are there any ghosts involved in this one?"

"How'd you guess?"

"I wish I could get that kind of help on my cases," he said.

The DHS guy who was skeptical said, "You really believe he talks to ghosts?"

"I don't know if he talks or just listens, but he gets information that could come from no place else," Eddie said.

"You know this for a fact?"

181

"The dead woman in his last case told him she had been murdered while the death certificate said natural causes. Once the bodies were exhumed they were found to be poisoned. I don't know how he could have known that from the information that we had, so yes I guess you can say I am a believer."

"So, you want in?"

"I think I will pass on this one. You have enough firepower to do the job without me. You did know that I am a lieutenant now."

"I didn't, but congratulations on the promotion."

"You get most of the credit for that. My bosses were really pleased by the way that case came to a close."

"If you help out with this one they might even make you a captain," I said.

"You know I would be there if you really needed me, but you have more than enough people to do the job. Besides, it's a federal case and it would be hard to justify my participation to the higher ups."

"You might get involved anyway if I can sweat some information out of these guys. I am investigating a five year old case of a young lady who disappeared from her apartment in Westlake. I have Dahari, the main guy here, and one of his underlings talking about it. They didn't use her name but indicated that they had fun before they killed her. Since they are from this area and probably know it better it is possible that they disposed of the body someplace nearby," I said.

"If you need help with that, yell. But I think I will pass on the current deal."

"I will get the vests back to you after this is over."

Chapter 21

Irvin called up a map on the computer when we learned that they were to meet at Denny's and he isolated the location on the satellite map. Man those things are great!

Instead of taking the two to Mustapha's house Dahari took them to his own, which was good from our point of view. We would at least know what they discussed while there.

Doug, Irvin and I went to the parking lot we had been using to monitor the bugs and stood around the car listening to the conversation the three carried on. Unfortunately we didn't get much at first as they spoke in Arabic.

After a few minutes they switched to English and talked about the coming mission.

"Do you think these guys are smart enough to do what needs to be done?" Dahari asked.

"They are not very smart, but I believe we can count on them to retrieve the packages and take them to the designated places. I am surprised that none even asked how they were to escape after they delivered the explosives. None of them are very devout and I know they would not go for a suicide mission. That's the reason we didn't tell them. Are you sure the remote devices will work?"

"Mustapha assures me that they will work fine. He has enough C-4 to act as the conductor for the signal. The only thing he is not sure about is the amount of damage the packages will do. We didn't test it so we will just have to take whatever happens. The limiting factor is how much he can get into each backpack without it looking suspicious."

"Are they going to be armed?"

"I haven't decided yet. On the one hand arming them would make it appear that they can kill more after the explosives detonate. On the other hand someone might detect the weapons and screw the whole thing up," Dahari said.

"Have you decided on a time yet?"

"I think just after noon tomorrow. The parks should be packed by then and give us maximum results."

"What did you do with the body of the girl Abdul asked you to take care of?"

"Dumped her in the woods in the mountains to the east. I have not seen anything in the papers to indicate that she has been found. The animals have cleaned her down to the bones by now," Dahari said.

"What about Ali? Is he over his sympathy pangs yet?"

"I believe so. He has gotten a job with a local bank and I don't have a lot of contact with him unless it is something Abdul wants done. He is going to pass the packages over the fence for the Somali's. He scouted the area both inside and out and thinks it will not be noticed."

"How many cars will be need tomorrow?"

"Three, and we will use our own vehicles to transport them. I suggest we not go to Mustapha's house until about 10:00 tomorrow. That way there will not be a lot of time for questions and second thoughts," Dahari said.

I was very happy to hear that conversation. If what they said about Ali was correct it shouldn't be hard to get him to reveal the location where they dumped the body. Of course if there was resistance tomorrow it might not matter.

Since we now knew the plan we called all the surveillance guys in for a briefing.

The house was not large enough to hold everyone at the same time so we went to the patio. The houses were far enough apart that the sound of our voices would not carry very far. I had my guys check to see if any neighbors were out and about before we started.

"There are three entrances to the house, front, back, and through the garage. The back is a sliding glass door so it will be a piece of cake going through that one. The front door is metal and will need a pretty good lick with a battering ram to tear the molding off. The garage door is the key. We don't want any of them anywhere close to the explosives. That door will need to be breeched first. It opens inward and I think Sam can probably take care of it with a shoulder. Those at the front and back will wait until they hear the commotion from Sam's efforts to take action."

"I am assuming that the explosives are not armed. It would be very foolish to do so in an area with so many gadgets that emit signals that could possibly detonate them. Garage door openers, key fobs, television signals, and short wave radios are only a few of the things that could ruin their day," I said.

"Doug, assign a man to the houses on each side and ask the occupants to vacate the house while this is underway. We will approach from the northern side of the house. Irvin has printed up some satellite maps that give you an idea of what you will be facing. The fence is redwood and will come apart easily, but I think we should have a couple of small ladders to assist us to the top. We can then drop down on the inside without making a lot of noise. If the gate is unlocked, which it was the last look we had, we will go through it. I want at least two men on the south side in case they try to break that way. No gun play unless they initiate it, and then shoot to kill. We can't afford to allow any of them to escape."

"The most important thing is the explosives. Sam will breech the door then James, Larry and I will go in right behind him. Any who try to escape through the garage will be taken under fire, armed or not," I finished.

"Questions?"

"What are we going to do with the live ones when this is over?"

"That is your bailiwick, but I would assume either city or county jail."

"Will all of these guys be armed?"

"I can't answer that. I know that at least four of them will be. Once any shooting starts you can't be too choosy about which ones have weapons and which don't."

"What's the timing?"

"Whenever Dahari and his two pals from Saudi Arabia show up. I imagine that will be in the neighborhood of noon."

"One other thing, and by no means the least important, be sure of your targets if we have to use weapons. The front entrance and the back patio door are directly across from each other, so be sure you don't shoot our own people."

I told Sam, "I'm going to leave Hakim here with Matt."

"I wondered what you were going to do with him," Sam replied.

There wasn't much to do now but wait for the night to pass.

I sent a two man crew back to check on Dahari. Maybe we could get some more juicy tidbits from the bug.

Dahari and the two talked a lot during the evening about how things were in Saudi Arabia and how the jihad was going in other countries.

Dahari's visitors felt more comfortable speaking Arabic and most of the conversation was in that language.

The only tidbit that we got was that Sarraf was planning an attack in either Paris or Rome. I assumed he wouldn't live long enough to put those plans into action.

Everyone met at the house the next morning. We had so many cars parked in the street that it must have appeared to the neighbors as if a party was going on.

We were far enough away from Ontario that we couldn't be sure to catch them at Mustapha's house if we waited until we got the word before we moved, so we drove to the area where he lived and used a mall parking lot to gather. It was within ten minutes of Mustapha's house and we could be sure of catching them all together.

The guys watching Dahari were supposed to call when he left the house. That call came at 10:30 a.m.

I told everyone to drive to the location and be ready for action. "Be sure you have the vest on," I cautioned.

Dahari and his pals drove right past the parking lot where we were waiting. The car following him was about a quarter of a mile back and they called to let us know that they would pass by us.

The chase car pulled into the parking lot and we went over the plan once more. "Okay," I said, "Let's get in position. Remember, the signal to breech the doors will be the sound of the garage door splintering."

Chapter 22

We all descended on the target, being careful to park far enough away to avoid attention.

The two who were going to clear the neighbors on either side went to the doors and rang the bell.

Soon I could see families moving to their neighbor's houses.

Once they had cleared the area I led the group to the house. The gate was unlocked and seven men moved to the back yard. The group who would breach the front door got into position. James had moved to the corner of the house to let me know when they were in position, and one of the HS guys stood at the back corner of the house to do the same for the group in the back yard.

Sam had padded his shoulder with a folded tee shirt and stood about three paces back from the side garage door. I listened but did not hear any noise coming from the garage. I gave him the signal and stood back out of his way.

When he hit the door it made a terrific racket as the door splintered and flew back against the wall.

I was in right behind him and James was behind me. Larry brought up the rear.

Mustapha was inside the garage with two of the Somali's fiddling with one of the explosive packages. I didn't hesitate. I shot Mustapha in the chest and one of the Somali's in the shoulder. James took care of the other one.

I could near the sound of panicked people in the house and stood with my pistol pointed toward the door into the house. Sam and James were checking the ones we had shot to make sure they were no longer a threat.

Mustapha was dead, as was the Somali that James had shot. The last was still moving and James found some wire and handed it to Sam, who wrapped it around the Somali's hands behind his back and gave it a couple of twists. I inventoried the explosives, thinking it might be a good idea to get them out of the house.

Gunfire was coming from inside the house, and a lot of it.

I told my group to stay put and watch the door. I then went back out to assess the situation. I didn't expect any of the bad guys to survive the initial charge but one of the Somali's was coming through the front door as I rounded the corner. I put two slugs into his body mass and that stopped him cold. I heard the stutter of an automatic weapon and heard screams. I continued to the front door, which was wide open. I could see one of the men from Saudi Arabia with an Uzi behind the couch. I took him out with a couple of more shots.

The gunfire ceased as suddenly as it had started. We went around checking each person who was down. Three of the HS people had wounds to either arms or legs. The vests saved a couple of others.

We provided first aid to our own people while some of us inventoried the terrorists. All of the Somali's were down but two of them would probably survive. Dahari lay in a pool of his own blood Mustapha and two Somali's were in the garage. The remainder was scattered around the living room, either dead or wounded.

Ali was the one I was looking for. I wanted him to lead me to Carolyn's body. I found him in the hallway with a bullet in his stomach. I grabbed a towel from the hallway closet and staunched the blood flow.

"Sam, call for some ambulances."

"Doug already did that," he replied.

"How many of ours got hurt?"

"Nobody real bad. A couple of HS guys got hit in the leg and shoulder. None of ours got hurt," he said.

"Make sure someone stays with the explosives until we can get a forensic team out here."

I found Doug and pulled him aside. "The press is going to be here before long. They monitor the emergency frequencies and when something like multiple ambulances are called they are right behind them. You are going to have to talk to them, so start composing your speech. You didn't call the Director yet did you?"

He shook his head negative. I think this might have been his first exposure to real people trying to kill him.

"I will make the call," I said.

I dialed her number and she answered on the first ring. She was quite obviously nervously awaiting the call.

"How did it go?" she said by way of greeting.

"We caught them all together. I think three or maybe four of them are still alive. Two of your people got hit in the shoulder and leg. The explosives are under guard and ambulances are on the way. The press will not be far behind. How do you want to spin the interviews?"

"What do you mean?"

"I mean do you want our involvement in the raid made public, or do you want me to give them the full story?" I asked.

"Since you were primarily responsible for running them down you should get the credit. You can tell them that you and your people were officially temporary Homeland Security agents. The rest of it you can give them the straight scoop. I will watch what the media says and call an official press conference to deal with the mass media. Let me say thank you for what you have done, just in case I forget to do so later," she said.

I heard sirens as the ambulances started to arrive.

I hung up the phone and met the first crew at the door.

"The ones still alive you can take to the hospital, but one of our guys goes along. The dead ones leave where they are lying until the forensics people finish with them," I said.

I went back to where Ali was lying. He was coherent, though obviously in pain. "I want you to show me where Carolyn Clayton's body was disposed of five years ago. I know that you, Dahari and Mustapha killed her after raping her. Will you show me where the body is?"

"Yes. It has bothered me ever since it happened. I was thinking about anonymously letting the police know about it, but I always backed out at the last moment. I will show you if I survive."

"Thank you," I said.

I called Irvin over and said, "Go with the ambulance that takes Ali to the hospital and take one of the HS guys with you. He is our only link to Carolyn now and I don't want anything to happen to him."

There were five people wounded so they called for additional ambulances. Before they arrived the press showed up. I got Doug aside and told him of my conversation with the Director. "You want me to do the initial interview?"

"It would probably be better if you do. This gunplay is not what it is cracked up to be. This is the first time I have used my pistol since I hired on."

"It doesn't get any easier. You just have to look at is as part of the job. James and I both have experience from the Middle East and it is still unnerving to have to use weapons. It will pass quickly when you come to the realization that you probably saved hundreds of lives by the action we took here."

Doug had called the county forensic team and they arrived shortly after the last ambulance left. Eddie Lopez, my contact with them was along in his own car. He heard about the action on the police radio and told his boss that he was going to the scene.

He joined me in the house where most of the bodies were and said, "Did you get them all?"

"All that we knew about. Come look at this," I said and took him to the garage."

"Wow. If they had been able to use all this they could have done a lot of damage."

"Who's in charge of the forensic team?"

"I guess I am the senior county guy," he said.

"You want everything left as is until they finish?"

"That would probably be best. They will chalk the outline of the bodies before they are removed."

The press was at the front door clamoring to be allowed inside, but two HS agents were keeping them out.

"I suppose I had better do the press thing," I said.

I went to the front door and addressed the half dozen reporters gathered there. "You will not be allowed in the house until the forensic team is finished with their job. I can give you a brief overview of what took place," I said.

John Buckner

One of the reporters from a local station said, "You're the guy who was involved with the mass shooting recently, aren't you?"

I smiled. "Yes, you have a pretty good memory. That was my people who were attacked at my house."

"What's the story here?"

"Let's get away from the door and I will give it to you the way it happened."

Once we moved to the sidewalk and they had their microphones and notepads ready I started the story.

"I was investigating a missing person from five years ago and came across some information that I thought concerned terrorists. I took the information to the Department of Homeland Security and they agreed with my assessment. Some more digging and a bit of luck identified Usha Bin Dahari as a contact here in the Los Angeles area. Once that happened I contacted the Director of Homeland Security again. Since my people had run down all the information we had, she suggested that we come to work for Homeland Security as temporary field agents."

"I agreed that was the best approach and she assigned additional HS agents for surveillance of the people we knew were involved. About a week ago five Somali citizens were infiltrated across the Mexican border and were delivered to one of the people we were watching here at this location."

"Mustapha, the guy who lives here, was putting together explosive packages for the five Somali's to detonate at Disneyland. That was to happen this afternoon at the busiest time."

"We had a force of 18 regular HS agents, plus five additional people who work for me. We followed Dahari to this house, which we have been watching for almost a month. The owner recently purchased so much fertilizer that his trunk wouldn't hold it all. I suppose you know that fertilizer is one of the ingredients used to make homemade bombs."

"We checked the premises while he was away and found the backyard chocked with weeds. The front lawn isn't much better, so the fertilizer was definitely not used on the property.

191

We now had three people who were connected with terrorism and five illegal Somali's at the same location. The conclusion was that they were getting prepared for a terrorist attack."

"We raided the house and a gun battle ensued. Two HS agents were wounded during the confrontation, and I believe seven or eight of the terrorists were killed. Three were wounded and taken to a hospital, escorted by HS agents. That's the short story."

"How did you come up with the information?"

"As I said, I was working on a missing person case from five years ago. The police did not have any leads and the parents of the missing person hired my firm to look into the matter. Her household goods had been packed up after the police investigation and stored in her parent's garage. We found the computer and asked if we might take it and see if there was anything of interest on it. From the files on the computer we learned that our missing person had been in Cannes, France the year before and had met someone new. She had taken a picture of him with another man. While going through the pictures someone recognized the other man as one of the London bombers from 2005."

"I provided that information to DHS and was asked to follow-up on their behalf. I eventually identified the main principle in the photo and through that association learned about the group of Somali's being infiltrated into the U.S. Someone, whose name I cannot mention, provided testimony that there was going to be a terrorist attack and he believed the target was Disneyland. Once the picture made sense we kept three of the local people under constant surveillance. One of the people visited what is known as a coyote, in L.A. That's someone who deals in the transport of human cargo from illegal border crossings to someplace else."

"When, two days later, the five Somali's showed up at this very house, we felt that was all the proof we needed to roll up the entire crew. When they all met here this afternoon it was obvious to us that they were preparing to carry out the attack. That was when we tried to arrest them."

"The rest as they say, is history."

"You sure seem to have a knack for solving mysteries. How do you account for that?" another asked.

"I guess I just dig deeper than those before me did. It's nothing magical. I just use common sense and try to run down every little piece of the puzzle that seems to fit with the case I am working on. I have good people working with me and we all share the same penchant for thoroughness."

"What have you worked on that the press isn't aware of?"

"Less than a month ago we had a convenience store owner who was losing a lot of money and couldn't figure out how. All his books checked out but the totals were not what they should be. He hired us and we investigated all the employees and even watched some of them away from work. We finally decided that the only way we were going to catch the culprit was through observation. One of my people spent the night in the attic of the store with enough of the tile in the drop ceiling removed to get a view and film whatever he discovered. We got the film of the transaction with his accomplice and turned the matter over to the police, who later arrested at least those two."

"I remember that. They didn't mention you at all in connection with that case."

"There was no need to. The police caught them red handed so my people wouldn't even have had to testify at the trial with things cut and dried."

"Did you give them a chance to surrender?"

I just looked at the guy like he was mad.

"If you were trying to avert a terrorist attack and you knew that there were at least eight terrorists inside a house, which also, I might add, contained enough explosives to level this entire neighborhood, would you give them a chance to surrender? Oh, I forgot to mention, they were armed with pistols and at least one automatic weapon."

"Doesn't the law force you to give them a chance to surrender? And what about a search warrant?"

"Gosh, I guess you got me there. I should have gone to the magistrate and gotten a search warrant, which would take me at least a couple of hours, in which time the bad guys would have leveled half of Disneyland."

"But you can't just circumvent the law," the same reporter said.

"I had just resigned from my temporary appointment as a HS agent when I noticed that the man I had been following was at this house. I added two and two and decided that it was my duty as an American citizen to stop a terrorist attack from occurring. Does that make what I did any more legal, or should I be arrested for breaking and entering, and possibly murder, because I definitely shot at least two of them, one as he was attempting to detonate the explosives he was assembling in his garage. I am sorry if you are morally outraged, but where I come from if you are dealing with snakes you don't give them a chance to bite you. You kill them. And these people were just a different breed of snake. The other side doesn't play fair, so we play by their rules."

"Then you think it is okay for private citizens to just break in on people and take their lives?"

"Mister, you are trying to put words into my mouth that didn't come out of it. What I said was that we had been watching these guys for almost a month and had documented proof that they were a terrorist group. When we realized that they were getting ready to act we stopped them. Now you can make of that whatever you want, but I have no regrets about what went down here today and if faced with the same situation tomorrow, I would react in the same manner."

"I imagine I make you uncomfortable by asking the tough questions," he said.

"You don't make me uncomfortable, you make me downright angry. Your questions are only intended to bait me into saying something that I shouldn't say and I resent your doing that. If you truly believe the drivel you are spouting makes you appear to be standing up for your fellow man I believe you are sadly mistaken. Your questions also lead me to believe that you do not have a very large following as a reporter."

"Next question," I said, looking at the rest of the group.

Nobody said anything.

"This might be against HS regulations but I want you guys to see just how close this neighborhood was to obliteration. Follow me.

I led them to the damaged side garage door so they could see inside. Mustapha's body was still lying as he had fallen, with the explosive package still in his grasp.

"If I had not shot that one he would have blown this entire neighborhood up."

The cameras flashed and the video tape got a good look at the carnage.

I led them back to the front of the house. "Now you are free to report this in any manner you choose. I would just appreciate it if you give all the facts when you do."

I tried to wrap it up but they wanted more.

"How is the case of the missing person going?"

"I'm sorry, but I can't talk about that without my client's permission. I will say that we now know that she is dead rather than just missing."

I called Doug up. "This is Doug Redmond. He is the senior HS agent on the scene. He might have something to add."

I went back into the house and called Harry Clayton.

"I just gave the news people some information that I probably shouldn't have. They are smart enough to track what I said back to a search for Carolyn. They will figure out who the missing person is and bombard you with questions. I am now very sure that Carolyn is dead. I might have a line on a way to recover her remains but I won't know for at least a week."

"I was just watching your live interview. Boy, you sure aren't very good at hiding your feelings," he said.

"Was it that apparent?"

"Yes but not in a bad way. I think you hit it on the head when you told the twerp that he was not much of a reporter. How long have you known they were planning this?"

"Since I got back from Saudi Arabia. By the way, I now have Hakim. I would like to bring him over to meet you folks tomorrow."

"Great. Just give us a call. Don't worry about the newshounds getting to us. I don't feel constrained to be nice to them."

I laughed. "I will call when things die down a bit here."

Chapter 23

The forensic team had been there for over two hours before they allowed the ambulances to take the bodies away. An explosive ordnance team from the FBI was called to take custody of the explosives.

My people had stayed in the back yard of the house, as had most of the HS agents, until most of the reporters left. It was almost dark before we managed to get away. I didn't trust Ali to live up to his promise to lead me to Carolyn's remains, so I wanted to go by the hospital to talk to him.

I called Irvin.

"I've been watching you on television for most of the afternoon. They keep playing your comments to the reporter over and over. I don't know if it's because they agree with what you said, or if they are trying to rake you over the coals," he said.

"How's Ali doing?"

"They operated on him to take the bullet out and he's in recovery. He will be doped up for quite some time I imagine."

"Sam and I are coming by in a few minutes, assuming I have the right hospital."

Irvin confirmed the address and we were there within half an hour.

I called Lillian on the way and she too had been watching the news. "I think you are going to be in such demand that people will hire you just to be able to say they know you."

"The other side of that is that the moral do-gooders will be on my case," I said.

"I don't think so. The film of the dead man in the garage with his hands on the explosives was very effective. Most people will realize just how close that situation was to being a real catastrophe," she said.

"I guess I can hope for the positive. Ali, one of the ones who was in on the murder of Carolyn, told me he would take me to the place where they disposed of the body. I hope he doesn't change his mind after he learns that he is not going to die right away. I want to get some directions from him before he realizes that he will be implicating himself in the murder if he takes me to the site. He just came out of surgery and will be doped up so I might be able to get it out of him before he regains all his faculties."

I got to the hospital and found Irvin sitting in the emergency waiting room.

"They're going to be taking him to a room soon. The doctor just told me about 30 minutes ago. He said the surgery went well and that he should recover fully."

"I don't care if he recovers or not, as long as I can get the information I need from him," I replied.

"Is the HS guy with him now?"

"Yes. They wouldn't let him in the operating room but he got to observe through the glass window."

"Let's tell him we are going to get something to eat. Then you can lead me to the cafeteria," I said.

"I haven't been there yet but we will find it," he said.

We ate a sandwich and went back to the emergency waiting room.

It was over an hour before the doctor came and told us that Ali was being moved to a room. "He is still heavily sedated but can respond to questions," he said.

We went to the room number the doctor had given us and met the HS agent at the door.

"Is he coherent enough to answer some questions?"

"He has his eyes open and seems to be somewhat aware."

I opened the door and went inside. I pulled up the room's lone chair to the bedside and he turned his head toward me.

"I need to know where you guys dumped Carolyn Clayton's body," I said without preamble.

"She was a lovely girl. I hated what we had to do to her," Ali responded.

"We will get to that later. Right now I need to know where the body is located."

"We drove east on Interstate 10 until we were almost to the mountains. I remember the last town we went through was Banning. It wasn't too far past that that we turned to the north and drove up into the mountains. There was a sign just before we got off the road that warned of flooding in the area in case of heavy rains. After we passed that sign it was not more than 200 yards that we turned off the road into the brush. We didn't get too far off the road because Usha was afraid of getting stuck."

"Is that where you three raped her?"

"Yes. Usha had a blanket in his trunk and we spread it on the ground. We had tied her hands behind her back but changed them to the front for the sex. One of us held her hands over her head while the others had her."

"How did she die?"

"Usha slit her throat after we had finished. He severed the jugular vein and she died very quickly. We rolled her body in the blanket and took her a bit farther into the woods. We didn't bury her, just dumped the body and left."

"Where did you pick her up?"

"At her apartment in the early morning hours."

"Did she put up a struggle?"

"Of course. Mustapha hit her pretty hard in the face and she lost consciousness."

"I suppose you took her car as well."

"Yes. It was a nice car and she had the title in the glove box. I sold the car to a Mexican in Riverside."

Irvin had been standing behind me with his laptop open and he handed it to me with the satellite map of Banning already cued up.

"Look at this map and see if you can identify the exit you took. This is the city limit sign for Banning to the east."

I held the computer so he could see the map. He looked carefully and pointed to the second major intersection outside the city limits. "I think this is the one. We just went straight until we were out of the housing area. The sign by the ditch was not too far from there."

I made note of the street after I gave the laptop back to Irvin.

I left the room and called the Westlake police department and asked to speak to Bill Hardwick. He wasn't in and I could not convince them to give me his phone number. "Will you call him and tell him that Bradley Kinkaid needs to talk to him about a case he is working on. It's the Carolyn Clayton disappearance if that helps."

I gave them my cell number and Irvin and I headed down to the lobby. Before we left I told the HS agent to call Doug and ask for someone to replace Irvin on the watch.

My phone chirped before we made it to the lobby. It was Bill.

"I think I might know where they stashed Carolyn's body. Do you want to take a ride with me tomorrow to Banning?"

"Yeah. I caught you on the news. They are playing that at every opportunity. Did you get the location from the terrorists?"

"Yes. Their boss in Saudi Arabia ordered the hit. He was responsible for the London attack in 2005. Carolyn had a picture on her computer of him and one of the London Bombers. That was the reason they killed her."

"Where do you want to meet in the morning?"

"Give me your number and I will look at a map and call you back," I said.

Irvin and I looked at the map again and decided that Riverside was the best place to meet. Irvin looked up the address for Denny's and I wrote it down.

I called Bill back and told him the address.

"You'd better wear some old clothing. I don't know what we will run into, but you can bet there will be bushes and briars."

When Irvin and I got back to the house everyone else was already there.

Sam was on the computer. "Man," he said, "You won't believe the number of hits on the web site. There were a few nastygrams, but more than 90 percent applauded your actions with the terrorists, and there are about 20 offers for our services."

"Anything that looked like it might be lucrative?"

"I didn't read them that closely. I was more interested to see how the general public was taking our confrontation with the terrorists."

"I guess Lillian was right. She said that the large majority would approve of the action we took."

"We got the location where they dumped Carolyn's body. It is just past Banning, which is a pretty good drive from here. Bill Hardwick is going to join us for a look at the location Ali gave me. I don't think he lied, though we might very well find nothing when we get there. Five years is a long time and predators would have stripped the bones clean in that time. We might possibly find some clothing remnants and a few bones."

"Who's going with you?"

"You, Irvin and Larry. James and Matt can stay here with Hakim and man the phones, or computer I should say."

I called Lillian to let her know that Ali had provided the location of the body. "I talked to Bill Hardwick, who is with the Westlake, P.D. I suspect that the remains, if we find them, are in San Bernadino County, so we will have that to deal with too."

We all turned in early. Tomorrow was going to be a very busy day.

Chapter 24

I had the group up and ready to go by 7:00 a.m. and we would fortunately be going against the traffic. It was still a hectic and slow journey.

Bill had not yet arrived at the Denny's so we got a large table and ordered breakfast. Sam ordered a double helping of everything.

When Bill arrived he joined us and placed his order. The rest of us had about finished and we drank coffee while Bill finished his food.

Irvin broke out the laptop and showed Bill where we thought Ali had directed us.

We had at least another hour on the road to get to the location. I volunteered to ride with Bill and Sam drove my car.

As we came into Banning I started looking for what Ali had explained to me. He said they took the second exit after they left Banning. That area looked too populated to me to have been the road they would have taken. I told Bill to go to the next exit. That one looked more like what I would expect. There was a housing development, but not a very large one.

We took the exit and headed north. The houses became scarcer as we headed up the hills. Soon the housing played out completely and a bit farther on I saw the sign about flooding that Ali had mentioned.

"He said that they turned off to the left within 200 yards of the sign we just passed," I said.

Bill spied what looked like an old trail that was overgrown with weeds. He parked the car beside the road and Sam pulled in behind us.

We all got out and headed into the woods. We walked perhaps 75 yards and came to an area that looked like what Ali had described. "Okay, fan out and look for scraps of clothing or bones," I said.

We formed sort of a circle and started making our way through the brush. It didn't take long. Irvin was the one who found her, and he called out to the rest of us.

What we saw was a rotted blanket and some pieces of clothing. Her skull and most of the larger bones were there, but the fingers and foot bones had been dragged away by some predator.

Bill said, "I'm out of my jurisdiction. I will call the San Bernadino sheriff's office and let them handle the forensics."

"I think I have the number programmed in my phone from the shooting incident on the freeway," I said.

I scrolled through the file until I found the number and hit the speed dial. I then handed the phone to Bill.

He identified himself and told what was needed. It would take them at least half an hour, probably more to get there, so we all went back to the cars to wait.

I took the opportunity to call Lillian. "Looks like the information Ali gave me was accurate. We found the remains and the San Bernadino Sheriff's deputies are on the way."

"It's sad that she is dead, but you and I already knew that, didn't we?"

"Yes we did. At least this will give the parents some closure. They will now know the truth. I hope the British take care of Sarraf. They hinted that they might. If he is still alive when this is over I might go back over there and take care of him myself."

"Don't tell that to just anyone," Lillian said with a chuckle.

"As they said in the old days, turnabout is fair play."

The county cars started showing up after just over half an hour. The first car contained two deputies. This was their beat and they had been given the location by the dispatcher. Soon another car with two people arrived, followed by the mobile crime lab.

Bill and I led them to the remains and backed off while the crime lab boys did their thing. They photographed the area where the body lay and the area where the assault probably occurred according to what Ali told me. There was obviously not going to be any evidence of the perpetrators with the body having lain there so long. They could get DNA samples and establish her identity I felt sure.

The next chore was not one I relished, but it had to be done. I gathered up my people and headed back to the house. I called the Clayton's enroute and told them I would be by later in the afternoon with Sam and Hakim. Roberta invited us to dinner and I begged off. I still had a lot to do, I told her.

"Hakim, you should be safe now. All your fellow countrymen are either dead or in the hospital. I will take you to the Clayton's later today. They will hire you to take care of the landscaping and provide you with quarters, and probably food. They will also pay you a decent wage."

"I cannot thank you and Mister Sam enough for what you have done for me," he said, tears filling his eyes yet again.

"We were just doing what was right. You helped us, so it is only fair that we help you."

I got yet another phone call, this time from Weatherly. "That was a good piece of work you and your folks did. I assume you got them all."

"All that we knew about, and if there are more they didn't associate with this group during the last month," I said.

"You have video and audio?"

"Yes but not the legal variety. Why the question?"

"I wonder if I might get a copy of any incriminating statements they made. It will help the Brits get off the dime with regard to Sarraf."

"They still haven't taken care of him?"

"I think the politicians are getting cold feet about it because he is part of the royal family."

"I may have to go back and do the job myself," I said. "There is enough on the audio recording to link them to the two who arrived from Saudi Arabia, you know the ones I got the pictures of in front of the mosque, and the pictures link them to Sarraf. We can't just let him continue his evil ways."

"Get me copies of the tapes and if that doesn't get them to act we will get together and come up with a plan to do it ourselves," he said.

Everyone present heard my side of the conversation.

Sam said, "Are you serious about going after Sarraf?"

"If nobody else will do it I believe we should. He will just set up another organization and pour money into it to take innocent lives. Do any of you have a problem with that?" I asked.

"Only about the legality of it," Sam said.

"It probably isn't legal, but I don't plan to get caught," I said.

"He is after all, a killer, and we have the evidence. Since we can't have him extradited the next best thing is that he have a fatal accident."

"It's something to think about," Sam said.

Sam, Hakim and I headed for the coast. We got to the Clayton's around 4:00 p.m. I introduced Hakim, who said, "I am pleased to make your acquaintance."

I asked Irvin to duplicate the tapes. I would call Weatherly tomorrow and see how he wanted to deliver them.

The Director of DHS had held a press conference the previous day and pretty much confirmed what I had told the reporters at the scene. She provided a lot more background and explained how I became involved in the affair.

As a final remark before taking questions she said, "If not for Bradley Kinkaid and his people we would now be dealing with the aftermath of one of the boldest terror attacks in history. The nation owes him a debt that can never be paid."

"Was his participation really needed once you knew who the terrorists were?"

"What if I were to say to you that you are no longer needed by your network because this news has already been reported? Or what if you were a baseball pitcher and had a no-hitter going into the ninth inning. You team is comfortably ahead but the manager decides that you are tiring and pulls you from the game. Those examples are not related to the matter at hand, but the principle is still the same. Brad had been running down the threads of the case for months and just when he identifies the bad guys we tell him thank you and we don't need you anymore. Extrapolate that to the public at large and how many private citizens do you think would even bother to report things that might really turn ugly," she said. "I deputized him because he and his people earned the right to follow the case through to the end. I might interject at this point that it was a sound decision. You all saw the pictures of the terrorist with his hand on the explosives. Had he been a second or two slower we would have had a catastrophe on our hands."

"But did he follow the protocols for law enforcement?"

"No he didn't. That is probably why he resigned his position before the action started. He knew that sworn agents would be bound by their oaths and he reasoned, rightly I might add, that the situation could not be handled in accordance with established police procedures. Let me give you another example. Suppose you are coming home from work and you find a mess in the house. Your teenage daughter is missing. You first call the police, then you look around to see if you find any clues to her whereabouts. You notice a strange car in the neighbor's driveway. While looking outside you see your daughter through the window of the house next door. You see a hand grab her and yank her away from the window. You have a pistol and go get it. Now you know your daughter is alive and in the house next door. You have a weapon and decide that you will have a better chance to rescue her than if you await the arrival of the police. The decision made you sneak onto the porch of the neighbor. Do you break the door down and confront the kidnapper, or do you wait for the police, knowing that the kidnapper could depart at any time, maybe taking your daughter with him, or maybe killing her before he retreats."

"Should he politely knock and say something like, 'I am the girl's dad, may I come in so we can talk this over. Or maybe you sneak under the window and get a peek inside. You have a clear shot at the kidnapper. Do you take the shot or say, come out with your hands up and I will not shoot you."

"I could give you many more scenario's that call for an instant decision, where lives are on the line, not only yours but others as well. Brad knew how many people were in the house and he knew that they were making preparations to take the bombs to Disneyland. Regardless of what the book says, he made the right decision and instead of being hailed as a hero, you people are getting hung up on law enforcement rules that do not apply to his actions. He knew the explosives were in the garage, and that was his major concern. Once the shooting started the others in the house started shooting. That was when my people started returning fire. Now can we move on to something else?"

The next question was, "You say he identified the terrorists. May I ask how he did that?"

"I might get the sequence of events confused because I am working from memory of what he told me. He had taken on a case to locate a young lady who had been missing for five years. The local police looked into the matter when it happened and had absolutely no clues. Brad and his people went over the police report and then the ladies apartment, which was now occupied by another tenant. When he asked his client about her furnishings he was told that they were packed up by movers and were still untouched in his garage."

"He took the computer and somehow managed to get access to it and her address book. Also on the computer was a diary the lady had kept since the year 2000. Now five years later she had a large file and part of that file was a narrative of an encounter she had while in Cannes, France on her graduation trip after college."

"There was a picture of the man and another, which one of the group recognized as one of the London Subway bombers. Remember this was five years later."

"At that point he called my office and said he had something we might be interested in. I sent someone to get a copy of the picture and made it available to the British authorities. I am not sure how he managed to get a line on one of the local terrorists, but he followed them everywhere they went for a long time. He also made that information available to me. He tied two other local people to the one he already had under surveillance and asked me for help keeping track of them."

"He made a trip to the Middle East and somehow learned that a terrorist attack was planned for the U.S. and that the target was Disneyland. You see, all he uncovered was because he was looking for the person responsible for the disappearance of a young lady. He didn't have to provide the information to us, but he did."

"Let me tell you this about Brad and his people. If I were a crook I would rather have the entire FBI, or Homeland Security for that matter on my case than have him looking for me. He is that good," she finished.

There were other questions but they were pure vanilla after recognizing that they had about all they were going to get.

Irvin was monitoring the web site. He said, "You won't believe how many hits we have gotten. It is in the thousands."

"Maybe we will get some work out of it," I replied.

"You already have offers for books and even a movie," Irvin said.

"You're serious?"

"Yep. This put us in the big time."

"Well Sam, Hakim and I are going to the Claytons to give them the news."

We drove to the beach and as we pulled into the driveway Harry opened the door.

"I am glad everything went so well. The Director of Homeland Security made you sound like Rambo, Chuck Norris, and John Wayne, all wrapped into one package. I don't imagine you will have to scrape the bottom of the barrel for work in the future."

"While I am happy with that development, I came to give you some sad news. One of the terrorists who survived gave me the location where they had disposed of Carolyn's body. I got a detective from Westlake to go with me to the site he had identified. We found the remains. The San Bernadino Sheriff's office is doing the forensics since it was in their jurisdiction. I have no doubt that it was her remains because they were exactly where the terrorist told me it would be. They will probably do DNA tests but at least you know the truth now."

"You know, there's a verse in the Bible, I believe it comes from the Book of John, Chapter 8, Verse 32. It was borrowed by the CIA and they use it as their motto. It goes 'you shall know the truth and the truth shall set you free'. I'm not sure it will set us free, but at least it will make life easier knowing the truth than to constantly wonder if she is alive and in some horrendous situation."

"I'm sorry it turned out this way, but I can empathize with your relief that you now know for sure."

"Come on in and let's tell Roberta."

We all went into the house and he called his wife into the sitting room. I went over the basics again for her benefit.

"Is there enough left to have a funeral?"

"Mostly bones, but I would say yes," I replied.

"You are absolutely sure it was her?"

"About as positive as I can be. One of the terrorists who was there gave me the exact location where the remains were found. I'm sure the police will do a DNA study to confirm it though."

Hakim had been standing silently through the exchange.

Roberta noticed him finally and smiled. "You have to be Hakim. We are looking forward to having you with us. I have had the small house out back made into living quarters. Why don't you have the gentlemen take you out so you can see it?"

I had the feeling that she wanted us out of the house before she broke down in tears. I grabbed Hakim's arm and we went outside, followed closely by Harry.

"It is hard on her. She has always held out hope that she was still alive," he said.

Hakim was amazed at the small house. It had one large room with a couch and a bed, a small kitchen and a bathroom.

"Is the nicest home I ever had," he said, breaking into tears of joy.

"You're going to have to get used to the tears," I told Harry. "He cries for joy, sadness, and anything in between."

I looked at Harry and thought I could see the shimmer of tears in his own eyes. "He may be just what we need," he said.

"The three that abducted her are all accounted for. Two are dead, and the snitch is in the hospital under guard. He will be tried for terrorist acts and will get a very stiff sentence. The guy who paid for the killing is still on the loose in Saudi Arabia. I thought the British were going to take care of him, and they still might. If they don't then me and the CIA will. I already have a promise for that."

"When I hired you I expected you to turn up some new facts, but the way this came about still boggles my mind. I think I agree with the Director of Homeland Security. If I was a crook I would rather have anyone other than you on my trail. I will give you a check now and we will call it square. Don't feel obligated to go to Saudi Arabia to take care of the vermin left."

"I am doing that for the world at large. He is the money behind terrorist acts and if we don't take care of him innocent people will die in the future because of our negligence."

We went back inside and left Hakim to marvel at his new home.

Roberta had herself under control when we got back inside.

"I'm going to have a funeral for her and I would like you and your friends to be there," she said.

"I would be honored, as would my friends," I said.

Harry went to the office and came back shortly with a check that he handed to me. I didn't even look at the amount, just folded it and put it in my shirt pocket.

"Hakim doesn't have anything other than the shirt on his back. I gave him some money, but I am not sure he will know how our economy operates. He will need some guidance," I said.

"Don't worry about him," Roberta said, "We will treat him as part of the family."

"I'm sure you will, and I thank you."

I stopped by Lillian's on the way back, although it was out of the way.

I rang the bell and she yelled for me to come on in. I had forgotten about the camera's we installed for her during the last case.

I opened the door and went inside.

Lillian sat at the computer. "You will never guess how many hits you have on your web site," she said.

"Well, I'm waiting," I said.

"Over half a million."

"Why would that many people access the site?"

"Probably because someone pasted it on Facebook, and you know how quickly that circulates around the world," She said.

"Have you sampled the comments?"

"Most applaud your action, but a few want to burn you at the stake for ignoring police procedures. You have offers for work, three for books, and one for a movie. It looks like you will not be eating leftovers for quite some time."

"I told the Clayton's that we had found Carolyn's remains, and dropped Hakim off with them. They made the shed in the back into a nice little apartment for him."

"So you are through with that case now?"

"Except for Sarraf. If the British don't take care of him I might have to go back and finish the job."

"Don't you have any qualms about doing that?" Merle asked.

"No. He is a murderer and his own government won't do anything about it. I talked with Weatherly from the CIA and he said if the British refuse to act that he will, with my help, of course. Harry Clayton wrote me a check before I left." I took it out and had a look. The check was for $50,000.

I handed the check to Lillian.

She whistled and handed it to Merle.

"I know how appreciative he is. Remember, I went through much the same thing. He just wants to show his appreciation for a job well done."

I didn't stay very long and was on my way home before the sun went down.

Chapter 25

The next day we started going through some of the e-mails. I asked Irvin to print them up so we could all take a batch and go through them. Even printing several on the same page he couldn't print all of them. When he had 500 sheets he divided them up. We were all present, so that meant about 100 sheets each.

Matt asked, "What are we looking for?"

"Job offers, and anything that catches your eye. Pull those sheets and lay them aside. We will all then look them over."

The job was tedious and time consuming.

I ran across one saying that with people like me around the country was going downhill and that what I did was completely unethical. The message said that he would rather deal with terrorists than people like me.

Most were positive, and the theme was the same for most of them. They said they did not see anything wrong with my actions based on the situation.

One was from a major publishing house offering to have someone ghost write a book about the events leading up to the final confrontation. They would pay a $100,000 advance against royalties.

Larry had one from a movie producer expressing an interest in doing a movie about the event. He didn't quote any figures but indicated that he thought a movie would gross 50 million.

There were job offers from all over the country and a couple of countries in Europe.

Some explained what they wanted to hire us for, but others apparently didn't want to put anything on the site for anyone to see and simply asked to be contacted.

People were wanting everything from searching for missing persons to finding lost animals.

By lunch time we had all made it through 100 pages each, which equated to more than 2,000 e-mails.

The most interesting ones, that is to say the ones offering opportunities for employment, we passed around while we were eating microwave lunches. None of us liked to cook, so that was our standard fare when we were at the house at meal time. "Put a check mark by the ones you think we should learn more about," I said.

I got a call from the Director of Homeland Security while we were eating.

"I have been told to offer you and your group employment with my organization. The thought was to keep your group together and assign you to the tough cases. The pay is not too bad. I can offer you a GS-15 position and your people GS-12. That equates to over $100,000 per year."

"I appreciate the offer, but what we do isn't about the money necessarily. If that was the motivation I have several offers for book deals and even one from a movie producer. I, and I believe most of my people, want to help people in need with no place else to turn to. And I don't believe any of us want to move."

"I was told to make the offer, and I have, so what's next for you?"

"I might need to go back to the Middle East. I talked to Weatherly yesterday and am passing the tapes and video on to him, presumably to pass on to the British. If they don't do something about Sarraf I am morally obligated to go after him. He was responsible for the death of my client's daughter and I can't see letting him walk on that count. He was also responsible for the London subway bombings and heaven knows how many more acts of terror. If he isn't stopped he will simply rebuild his organization. There's no shortage of Islamic zealots in the area."

"I will tell my boss that I made the offer and you turned it down. I won't go into your reasons. If you need anything from me just call."

After we hung up I told the guys about the check from Clayton. "He had agreed to spend that much trying to find out about his daughter, so he went ahead and paid it all."

"We were offered jobs with Homeland Security at an annual wage of over $100,000. We would have to move to the

Washington area, and I turned that down as well. Do you guys agree with those decisions?"

Everyone either nodded or said yes.

"We have enough job offers to keep us busy for the foreseeable future," Sam said, "and I like the way we operate. I don't believe we would have the same freedoms if we went to work for the government."

Matt said, "Yeah, and we work well together. Everyone has a say and does what needs to be done without any hard feelings. I don't believe we would find that if we had to answer to the next higher in the government hierarchy."

"What do you guys think about the book offers?" I asked.

Irvin said, "I kind of like the idea. We will have a forum for getting our side of the story to the general public."

"And the movie offer?"

"Same with that. If we have a say in the way they put the movie together it will make a lot of money."

"Let's let both of those things simmer for a couple of days. I think we should find our next job from the inquiries we have."

"What are we interested in? Missing persons, unsolved murders, or what?" James asked.

As we all looked at the items offering work one entry caught my eye.

I picked it up and read the short paragraph.

"This looks interesting," I said.

"Which one is that?" Irvin asked.

"The one about the haunted house," I said.

"Why don't you read it aloud so we all know what you are talking about?

I read the e-mail aloud. It said, "I have been watching the news about what you did in California. From what I have learned you have a top notch team and get results. The problem I have is that my house is inhabited by ghosts. I have had psychics, exorcists, and exterminators try to get rid of them but to no avail. I am very wealthy and don't get along all that well with those who will by default become my heirs. I don't really believe in ghosts, but unless my kin are doing something to speed me onto the other side I have no explanation for what is happening. If you think you might be able to help me with the problem call me and I will make arrangements for you to come see me. I will of course pay you for your time and expenses. Call me at the number below to either accept my invitation or tell me you are not interested. I think this is a case that might intrigue you."

The person did not give a name and all we had was the phone number and his e-mail address.

"That is really weird," Larry said.

"Do you think he knows about Lilian, or you for that matter?" Sam asked.

"I suppose it is possible, though I don't remember mentioning anything about it to the media. One way to find out," I said taking out my phone.

I dialed the number from the message and a female answered the phone. I assumed she was the maid and said, "May I speak with the gentleman of the house?"

"Who shall I say is calling?"

"Brad Kinkaid from Los Angeles."

"Will you hold please?"

In a minute or so the phone was picked up someplace else.

"Ah, Mr. Kinkaid, so glad to hear from you."

"I was rather intrigued by your e-mail. What area of the country do you live in?"

"I am in New York at present. The house to which I referred in the message is in Rhode Island. My name is William Perkins. Just call me Bill."

"Why do you think your house is haunted?"

"Because strange things happen there."

"Can you give me some examples?"

"Things that go bump in the night. I mean doors slamming, lights coming on by themselves, strange breezes, as if someone just passed close to you, things like that."

"How old is the house?"

"It goes back to revolutionary days. I think it was actually built before the Declaration of Independence was signed. It's near the seashore and is registered with the National Historic Society."

"What exactly do you want me to do?"

"Spend some time at the house and tell me if my potential heirs are messing with my mind, or if there really are ghosts in the house. I would prefer that it be the former because the other option is too hard for me to believe. Having said that, I don't see any way any of my kin could be responsible."

"Why specifically did you call me?"

"Well the reason was two-fold. I wanted to reward you in some way for the job you did on the terrorists, and after the build-up the Director of Homeland Security gave you I reasoned that anyone who could do what your firm did with little or no information might be able to get to the bottom of my problem."

"If I agree to have a look at the house it will be expensive. I have six people who will need to accompany me, and if possible we would all like to stay in the house, probably as long as a week."

"Money is no object. Bring as many as you need."

"When and where can we meet?"

"If you will make arrangements to fly into Providence I will have someone meet you and bring you to the house."

"Let me talk it over with the others and I will get back to you, probably later today or early tomorrow morning."

"Thank you very much for what you did to keep our country safe, and for agreeing to look into something that you probably don't believe."

"I might be more open minded than you think concerning the departed."

"Can you explain that in clearer language?"

"I will wait until we meet if you don't mind."

After I hung up I said, "I don't believe he has any idea about what Lillian can do."

"It's the fickle finger of fate rearing his ugly head," James said.

"I want to make sure Lillian wants to go along," I said and dialed her number."

"Lillian," I said when she answered, "how would you like to take a vacation to the east coast?"

"What's the catch?" she asked.

I told her about the phone call from Perkins.

"He had not heard anything about our ghosts?"

"He gave no indication that he had. The reason he gave was to reward me for taking care of the terrorists, and the build-up I got from the Director of Homeland Security. He is apparently very wealthy and agreed to foot the bill for the entire crew to fly to Providence," I said.

"When are you thinking of leaving?"

"Probably tomorrow or the next day," I replied.

"Okay, count me in. Is Merle invited too?"

"Of course."

"This sounds intriguing, if what he told you is true."

After I hung up I said to Irvin, "Get on the internet and make us all reservations to Providence, Rhode Island."

"Early enough to get there before dark. We will probably need to catch a commuter flight to Providence from New York or Boston."

I was much like Lillian. I was intrigued by the thought of ghosts spending their time in a single house.

We left the next morning just after 9:00 a.m. We flew to Boston and caught a commuter flight to Providence as I suspected we would have to do.

When we arrived in Providence a liveried chauffeur was holding a sign with my name on it.

I identified myself and he led us outside. I was somewhat worried that there would not be room for all of us, but he led us to a stretched limousine and we all fit comfortably.

"I was told to take you to the house. Mr. Perkins will join you there tomorrow. The kitchen is well stocked so help yourselves to whatever you want."

He drove for almost half an hour and we entered the seaport town of Newport. He then took a road along the coast and we started to see large houses on huge lots. I suppose mansions would be a better description. None was less than 10,000 square feet by my estimation.

He turned into a driveway and used a remote to open the gate. The house was really huge and sat on at least ten acres.

The chauffeur stopped in front of the house and unlocked the door. We only had carry-on bags and we grabbed those and followed him into the house. The exterior was stone and the inside was hardwood everywhere, with area rugs and runners.

"How many bedrooms?" I asked.

"Eight, I believe. Just settle in wherever you are comfortable."

He went to the kitchen and asked if we knew how to operate all the appliances.

"Mr. Perkins asked me to say he will join you between nine and nine thirty tomorrow."

When the chauffeur had left I asked everyone in general, "What would something like this cost?"

"More than we have," Sam replied.

Lillian was a bit more knowledgeable about the area and told us that the area was known as 17 mile drive and all the houses dated back to revolutionary days, at least they wanted everyone to think they did. The prices were in the millions and any that went on sale only lasted a short time.

I walked outside and Sam joined me, along with Irvin. We surveyed the property and walked along the fence line all the way around the house. The lawn was well kept and there was a small garage in the back to house the tools and equipment.

"Are we looking for something in particular or just exercising?" Sam asked.

We were nearing the back of the lot and came upon a small graveyard. The house blocked the view of it from the road, but there were several tombstones.

I looked at the inscriptions, mostly to get an idea about how old they were. The dates indicated that the house did indeed date to the revolutionary war. The oldest of the graves was dated 1794. It had the name Cyril Perkins engraved on it. The others brought the time element to 1914. That was the newest of ten graves.

Sam said, "If the house has ghosts I'll bet they come from these graves."

"At least it's not a long commute," Irvin said.

We all got a good laugh out of that.

When we got back to the house I told Lillian about the graves and how far back they went.

She was thoughtful for some time. "I wonder why 1914 is the latest. Surely some of the family has died in the interim."

Lillian rummaged around in the kitchen, and with Merle helping they made spaghetti and a large salad.

We ate at the dining room table and sat around talking afterward.

"I have a nagging feeling that the graveyard in back has something to do with our problem," I said.

"I do as well but I have no idea how," Lillian said.

Merle had not said much but now agreed with Lillian and me.

I asked the others, "Did any of you get the feeling that the graveyard out back it the cause of the problem?"

All shook their heads negative.

Lillian said, "It could be that only those who have interacted with ghosts can feel the attraction."

We talked for a while longer and turned in fairly early.

I slept fitfully. I heard strange noises that might have been coming from the other rooms, or might have been ghosts. I was not sure what to make of it until my door opened and the ghost of a woman dressed in clothing from the 1800 time frame appeared.

"Tell William to bring our relatives back."

"Back from where?" I asked.

"From other graveyards," she said, and faded out.

The door still stood open, so I knew I wasn't dreaming.

I got up and closed the door and went to the bathroom.

I laid back down and thought about what had happened. Was this going to be as simple as exhuming graves and reburying them here?

I wondered why others had been buried elsewhere when there was ample room in the plot out back for many more graves.

I fell asleep and slept soundly until morning.

I was the first one up and went to the kitchen to make coffee.

Lillian joined me before the coffee finished.

"Did you have any visitors last night?" I asked.

"You too?" she asked.

"Who was yours and what did they want."

"It was an older man. He didn't identify himself but said that William was being stubborn and that I should convince him to bring their relatives back."

"I had a middle aged woman dressed in old clothes and she told me essentially the same thing."

"You don't suppose they think their relatives are still alive?" she asked.

"I took it to mean that those buried elsewhere should be relocated," I said.

"That would seem to be the more likely request."

"On the other hand, there are only about ten graves in the cemetery and there have surely been many more than that in the family line since 1794, so what does that mean?"

"Without some amplification we are not going to know," Lillian said.

She started to scramble eggs and cook bacon while I toasted an entire loaf of bread.

"Goodness that's enough to feed an army."

"But just the right amount to feed Sam," I said laughing.

I guess the smell of bacon and eggs cooking permeated the house because by the time we finished the cooking everyone was up.

Once we were seated I asked, "Did any of you have any strange things happen overnight?"

Sam said, "My door was opened but I didn't see anyone."

Irvin said, "I heard the door open and close. Then I heard water running in the bathroom. I just assumed it was one of you."

John Buckner

Matt said, "I think I saw a ghost. My door was standing open when I awoke and I saw something sort of opaque. It didn't have much form and finally just vanished."

I told them about my encounter and Lillian did the same.

"They were two different Ghosts?" Sam asked.

"Yep, one male and one female."

"I saw the one Lillian saw, though I didn't hear the conversation," Merle said.

"So what does it all mean?" Irvin asked.

"I think that those in the family who died after 1914 were laid to rest elsewhere and they want them to be moved to the cemetery out back. We will probably need additional clarification to substantiate that premise, but I think they will appear again," I said.

The front door opened and William Perkins came into the dining room.

"You I know from television," he said to me.

We shook hands and I introduced everyone else.

"Did you have a restful night, or did the ghosts hinder your sleep?"

"How many of your relatives have died since 1914?" I asked.

"Let's see, my grandfather Perkins died in 1938. My grandmother, his wife, died in 1946. They only had the one child, my father, and he died in 1982. That's it for the Perkins side of the family. I don't have any children. On my departed wife's side there are several nieces and nephews but I don't know much about her family tree," he said. "Why the questions about my family history?"

"It has to do with your ghost problem. It seems those buried out back are lonely for their kin and want them to be moved to the private cemetery"

"How do you know this?"

"Because ghosts appeared to Lillian, Merle and myself last night and told us," I said.

"You're serious! You actually saw the ghosts?"

"Let Lillian give you a bit about her background," I said.

221

Lillian started out with her educational background and told about the early incidents she had witnessed. She carried the story through to the present time.

"That's part of what makes Brad and his crew so successful at solving crimes. The spirits, once they make contact seem to keep an eye on what the contact does afterward, and if they can help with something they make an appearance."

"Ghosts have been part of every case I have worked on. They don't do anything overtly, but drop a name, or say that I am looking in the wrong direction. That's how I got the name of the terrorist in L.A. to start to build files on all of them. Lillian seems to get the same sort of guidance and the ghosts never give us any information that isn't directly related to the case we are working on," I said.

"I am having a hard time believing this," he said.

"The solution is fairly simple. Just locate the graves of your ancestors and have them reburied in the back yard. The ghosts will then be at peace and stick to their own kind."

"I mean that you communicated with ghosts."

"Well you knew they were here. That was the reason you called me," I said.

"Yes, but I was hoping you could come up with some alternative solution," he said.

"Well, I gave you the alternative solution. Dig your ancestors up and replant them in the back yard."

"You aren't just having fun with me are you?"

"Where ghosts are concerned it is no laughing matter," Lillian said.

"You are sure it is the ghosts of my ancestors?" he asked.

"Very sure. The way they were dressed and what they said they wanted makes it airtight," I said.

"I don't have any idea where some of them were buried," he said.

"If they lived in this area it is probable that they are in a cemetery nearby. It shouldn't be too difficult to find the graves."

"Why would they not have appeared to me and told me the same thing?" Perkins asked.

"Probably because you don't believe in ghosts. They don't appear visually unless it is to one who believes in the phenomenon," I said.

"Can you locate the graves and have them moved here?"

"I can, but you could probably do that on your own," I said.

"I would rather have you do it if you have the time," he replied.

"If that is your wish."

"It is. I don't want anything to do with ghosts. I would like to accompany you on the search though."

"I will need names of all who have died since 1914."

"That will only be four people. My grandfather and grandmother, then my mother and father."

Irvin got on his computer and located the cemeteries in the area. Bill knew where his parents were buried so we only had the grandparents to worry about.

Irvin got the addresses of the local cemeteries and we left the house around 10:00. The first place we checked turned out to be where the grandparents were buried. We found the office and inquired about having the remains transferred to a private cemetery.

"Do you want anything special in terms of a service at the place where they will be replanted?" the manager asked.

I looked at Bill and he shook his head no.

"Just dig them up and move them to the new location," I said.

"When do you want it done and where will they be relocated to?"

"A private residence along the coast. I would like you to have your grave digger prepare four new graves. What's the address Bill?" I asked.

He gave the cemetery manager the address.

"That's along the coast, isn't it?"

"Yes," Bill replied. "The house is one of the older ones."

"I can have the backhoe out there this afternoon if it will fit your schedule," he said.

"We should be back there by midafternoon. Have the digger show up around two," Bill said.

We drove to the cemetery where Bill's parents were buried and did the same thing.

Over the next three days the task was completed.

The ghosts showed up the night after we made arrangements for the bodies to be moved. The woman visited Lillian and the old guy visited me.

We both told them that arrangements had been made to have their kin next to their graves.

On the third day the four caskets were delivered and placed in the new graves. The graves were then filled in and the extra soil hauled away. The markers had been repatriated and would be placed once the ground was prepared.

We had no further instances of the ghosts appearing after that. Perkins stayed in the house with us and seemed relieved that our suggestion seemed to placate the ghosts.

At breakfast the day after the caskets were placed in the new graves, Perkins handed me a check for $50,000. "That will take care of your expenses and I can't tell you how relieved I am about the house. I was to the point that I hated to stay here overnight."

Irvin made reservation for us via New York and we were back home just after dark.

Epilog

Weatherly called the day after we got back.

"Looks like we don't have to worry about Sarraf. It seems someone gunned him down in front of his mosque. The authorities have no suspects," he told me.

"That's good. I didn't really want to go back over there."

I told the others the good news, and we got back to looking at the e-mails.

There were more job offers than we could count, and some of them were from foreign countries. Ironically, we even had an offer from Saudi Arabia.

When we went to the Clayton's to give them the news about Sarraf we checked in on Hakim. He was as happy as a kid in a candy store. Harry said he was a tireless worker and assured us that they would take care of him.

The last loose thread was tied up and we could now move on to other things. Our problem now was not finding work, but deciding which offer to take. I signed on with a major publishing house to do the book.

It didn't appear that there would be any repercussions about the way we handled the terrorists, and the event was becoming old news.

Our major problem now was deciding which case to work on next.

www.ingramcontent.com/pod-product-compliance
Lightning Source LLC
Chambersburg PA
CBHW070815120626
46556CB00002B/511